"We didn't get off to a very good start this morning. Let's start over.

"I'm Turk Garrison. I'm new in town and looking for someone to show me around. Wanna volunteer? I promise I don't bite, scratch or drool in public. So whaddya say? Are you game?"

Unable to take her eyes off his engaging smile, Rachel tried hard not to be charmed. She wanted to say yes so badly she could taste it. Instead she said, "No."

If he hadn't been so damn sure of himself—not to mention boyishly attractive—she might have said yes. But a woman only had to glance over at him to know that he was trouble any way you looked at it.

"Hey," Turk said, grinning, "that's okay. I'm a patient man. And it's not like I don't know where to find you.

"After all…you're right next door."

Dear Reader,

People always ask me where I get my stories, and my answer is always the same: They float around in the air. People tell me that I hear or see something that triggers an idea, and suddenly, the story is there. This particular book was told to me by different people at different times. Years ago, I heard about a woman who wasn't looking for love, just a doctor to father her baby. She really did go to a bar near the medical center and had a one-night stand with a doctor. When she got pregnant and had the baby, she never told the father of her child.

That woman, whose name I never knew, became my heroine, Rachel Martin. The rest of her story is based on another true story. Somewhere in south Texas, there is a woman who married a man who had a vasectomy without telling her. She, too, desperately wanted a baby and didn't know for years that that was never going to happen.

I wanted more for Rachel Martin. Determined to get the baby she wanted at all cost, she thought she had everything worked out. Then Fate moved in next door. Don't you just love that?

Enjoy!

Linda Turner

Linda Turner

MISSION: M.D.

Silhouette®

Romantic

SUSPENSE

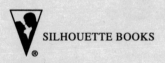 SILHOUETTE BOOKS

ISBN-13: 978-0-373-27526-7
ISBN-10:   0-373-27526-9

MISSION: M.D.

Books by Linda Turner

Silhouette Romantic Suspense

*Gable's Lady #523
*Cooper #553
*Flynn #572
*Kat #590
Who's the Boss? #649
The Loner #673
Maddy Lawrence's
    Big Adventure #709
The Lady in Red #763
†I'm Having Your Baby?! #799
†A Marriage-Minded Man? #829
†The Proposal #847
†Christmas Lone-Star Style #895
**The Lady's Man #931
**A Ranching Man #992
**The Best Man #1010
**Never Been Kissed #1051
The Enemy's Daughter #1064
The Man Who Would
    Be King #1124
**Always a McBride #1231
††Deadly Exposure #1304
††Beneath the Surface #1321
††A Younger Man #1423
††Mission: M.D. #1456

*The Wild West
†The Lone Star Social Club
**Those Marrying McBrides!
††Turning Points

LINDA TURNER

began reading romances in high school and began writing them one night when she had nothing else to read. She's been writing ever since. Single and living in Texas, she travels every chance she gets, scouting locales for her books.

Prologue

The phone rang promptly at eight o'clock, just as Rachel Martin had expected. Grinning, she snatched it up without bothering to check the caller ID. "Hi, Lily. You're right on time as usual."

"Hi, Rachel."

Surprised, she almost dropped the phone. "Natalie? Is that you? I was expecting Lily."

"I'm here," Lily said with a chuckle.

"Me, too," Abby chimed in cheerfully. "We wanted to surprise you with a conference call."

"Well, you certainly did that," she retorted, smiling. "What's going on? I know a conspiracy when I smell one. What's up?"

"I want you to be in my wedding," Natalie said.

"Me, too."

"Ditto."

Stunned, Rachel felt as if the three of them had just reached through the phone and knocked her off her feet. "All three of you are getting married?"

Lily laughed at her shocked gasp. "It's crazy, isn't it? I didn't think I'd ever be happy again, and then almost overnight, everything changed."

"I took one look into Logan's eyes and it was all over," Abby added. "Of course, I didn't tell him that. I didn't even tell myself."

"But then you realize that even though you're scared of making another mistake, you don't even want to think about living without him," Natalie said huskily. "I think Max was just as stunned as I was when he asked me to marry him."

"But you didn't give him a chance to take it back, did you?" Lily teased. "I didn't with Tony, either."

"So will you do it?" Abby asked Rachel. "Will you be in our weddings? We need you. This all started last summer. Remember? When we all sat around at our class reunion, talking about how miserable we were?"

"So we changed our lives and found the happiness we'd always been looking for," Lily said. "You have to be a part of our weddings, Rachel. We all encouraged one another that day. The four of us have to stick together."

"But nothing's changed in my life," she replied. "I still want a baby. Just a baby. No husband. No one to lie to me and pretend he wants the same thing I do."

"Not everyone is like Jason," Abby pointed out quietly. "There are good, honest men out there. I know. *We* know. We all found one."

"They're out there," Lily told her. "You just have to give yourself a chance to meet one."

"No," she said flatly. "I can't. I'll never trust a man again."

"Oh, sweetie, don't say that!"

"It's the truth," she retorted. "You know how much I wanted a baby. I spent years trying to get pregnant. And all the time, Jason knew it was never going to happen. Do you have any idea how devastated I was when I found out he'd had a vasectomy before we got married? I cried in his arms every time I had a period! How could I have been such a fool?"

"Don't you dare beat yourself up for what that man did," Natalie said. "He was the fool, Rachel. Not you."

"That's right," Abby said, "You'll make a wonderful mother. Go have a baby if you want one. You don't need a man for that—just his sperm."

"Go to a sperm bank in Austin," Lily suggested. "You can pick out the height, coloring and intelligence of your baby's father and never have to even meet him. Of course, you won't get any financial support and you'll have to go through the pregnancy alone, but we'll be there for you. And you make good money with the bakery, don't you? You can do this, Rachel."

"At least you won't have to worry about someone you want no part of having an influence on your child," Natalie said. "If you're sure you just want a baby and no father to go with it, then a sperm bank would be the way to go."

They weren't saying anything she hadn't thought of herself, but something squeezed her heart at the idea of lying on an examining table and being impregnated so impersonally. "I don't know if I could do that," she admitted honestly. "It just sounds so…"

"Clinical?" Lily supplied for her. "You're right. It does. But if you don't want a man…"

"Just because I can't trust a man enough to have one in my life doesn't mean I can't get pregnant by one…then walk away."

Silence fell like a stone. "I've surprised you," she said quietly.

"Could you do that?" Natalie asked, curious. "*Could* you meet a man, have sex with him and get pregnant, then just walk away?"

For the last few months, Rachel had asked herself that same question more times than she could count. And the answer was always the same. "I don't know," she said honestly. "I guess we'll find out."

Chapter 1

Standing before the large round mirror of her antique dresser, Rachel studied herself with a critical eye. She never had been what she would call a girlie-girl. She couldn't remember the last time she'd painted her fingernails, and she wasn't one of those women who spent hours in front of the mirror, messing with her hair. Half the time, she twisted it up on top of her head, clipped it out of the way, and walked out the door without even looking at it twice. Lipstick was an afterthought, perfume was the smell of sugar and yeast that clung to her from the bakery. She wore jeans and a baker's smock to work, and given the chance, tennis shoes.

So how was she supposed to dress to attract a man? she wondered wildly. It had been so long since she'd had a date that she didn't even know where to begin.

More blush, she decided, frowning at her pale, reflected image. She needed more color in her face…and jewelry. Her neck looked bare, her earlobes naked. What did the kids call it now days? Bling-bling. That was what she needed. All she had, however, was a simple gold locket that her grandmother had given her. Would that date her? Or make her look like some kind of innocent who'd been living in a convent?

Undecided, she slipped it on, then added blush to her cheeks and painted on red lipstick. Stepping back, she frowned at her reflection. The woman who stared back at her in the mirror was a stranger. Dressed in red, her dark hair tumbling around her shoulders, she looked hot, sultry, sexy.

It was the dress, she decided. There was no question that it was designed to appeal to a man. It hugged her slender figure and ever so slightly dipped between her breasts, revealing just a hint of cleavage. Paired with strappy, spiked sandals, the dress gave her the look of a woman on the prowl.

Suddenly having second thoughts, Rachel seriously considered chickening out right there and then. Maybe Abby and Lily and Natalie were right. There was another way to have a baby. What difference did it make if she actually met her baby's father? It wasn't as if she would have a chance to learn that much about his character. She was never going to see the man again.

She wanted a baby, not a relationship, she reminded herself. And with a sperm bank, she wouldn't have to worry about some man calling all the time, wanting to get to know her—and his baby—better. All she wanted was his sperm. So what if it was clinical? What could be more clinical than picking a stranger out of a bar to be the father of her baby?

Don't second guess yourself now, a voice in her head warned. You don't have a lot of choices here, you know. Unless you want to get pregnant the old-fashioned way—by a man you fall in love with— you've only got two options. The sperm bank or seducing a stranger. If you want to know for sure that the father of your baby is not only intelligent, but a kind and caring man, then don't you think you'd better meet him face-to-face?

Her heart stopped dead at the thought. Could she really pull this off? What if he guessed what she was up to? Any man in his right mind would be furious, and she couldn't say she'd blame him. She intended to use him in the worst way a woman could use a man, but she truly had no other choice. She'd already tried the fairy tale, love and marriage, but there'd been no baby to make three.

And during the years of their marriage, Jason had made sure that she'd known who was to blame for that. *She* was the one whose hormones were out of whack. *She* was the one who was somehow deficient and didn't have what it took to have a baby. And she'd believed the lying jackass.

The day she'd discovered the truth, she'd walked out. How could she have loved a man like that and never realized what a monster he was? How could she have been so blind? She'd promised herself then that she was done with men, with lies, with trust. Never again would she place her hopes and dreams in anyone else's hands but her own.

She wanted a baby, and she didn't have a clue how long it would take to get pregnant. Months? Years? The constant tick of her biological clock echoed in her ears at the thought. The women in her family had all gone into menopause by the time they reached forty. If she ran out of time…

Pain squeezing her heart at the thought, she grabbed her purse and turned her back on the woman in the mirror. When she locked her front door and slipped behind the wheel of her VW Bug a few minutes later, she tried to convince herself she was doing the right thing. All she had to do was shut her brain and conscience off and go after what she wanted. Other women did it all the time. So could she.

Of course, she'd been telling herself that for months, long before Lily and Natalie and Abby had called last week and asked her to be in their weddings, and she'd yet to do anything. And who could blame her? She was going to have sex with a stranger in order to get pregnant! And that wasn't something she did lightly. On top of that, the father of her child had to be someone special. Someone who was caring and kind and smart, someone any child would love to claim as his father. And she'd decided there was only one place where she could find such a paragon…in a hospital. The father of her child needed to be a doctor.

Still, even after she'd come to that conclusion, she'd done nothing. Then she'd turned thirty-five on Monday, and she'd felt time slipping through her fingers, time she would never get back. And she'd known she couldn't wait any longer. She had to do something. Now.

The man she was looking for wasn't in Hunter's Ridge, Texas. The town was too small, barely eight thousand people, and ever since she'd moved there five years ago and started running her grand-mother's bakery, she'd met just about every inhabi-tant of the place. The only doctors in town were pushing retirement and happily married to little white-haired old ladies. If she wanted to find someone, she would have to go into Austin.

The city was forty miles and a world away. No one knew her there, but her pounding heart took little comfort in that as she drove toward the city lights. She was about to make one of the most important moves of her life, and she was a nervous wreck. Her palms were sweating, her mouth dry, and every instinct she had urged her to turn the car around and race back to Hunter's Ridge. In her head, however, she could hear her biological clock ticking. Her chin set at a determined angle, she headed for the medical center.

The bar she chose was trendy and popular, and a friend who was a nurse had told her that if she wanted to meet a doctor, this was the place to go. It was one of the favorite watering holes of residents and medical students alike. As Rachel pulled into the parking lot, she could well believe it. She couldn't find a single parking space and had to park on the street.

Cutting the motor, she stepped from her car, her heart skipping every other beat. It was game time, she thought grimly. No more excuses, no more procrastinating. If she really wanted a baby, this was her chance. All she had to do was walk inside the bar and find a man who met her requirements for a father, then seduce him.

It should have been easy. The second she walked through the front door, she drew every male eye in the place. All she had to do was smile, find a seat at the bar and wait for someone to join her.

She didn't have to wait long. "Hey, sweetheart," a tall, dark-haired man greeted her with a leering grin as he sauntered up to the bar. "I bet you could use a drink. Bartender, the lady would like a beer."

Taking a position just inches away from her, he never touched her, but he didn't have to. He stroked her with his eyes, letting his gaze dip to her breasts, the curve of her waist and hips, then focusing on her mouth in a way that made Rachel's skin crawl.

Just barely suppressing a shiver of distaste, she said, "Thanks, anyway, but I don't like beer."

"No problem," he said smoothly, his eyes once again dropping to her breasts. "I appreciate a lady with class. How about a glass of wine? Champagne? You name it, it's yours."

She could have him if she wanted him—the offer was right there in his beady little eyes. *Okay, here's your chance,* the irritating voice of reason drawled mockingly in her head. *Just how desperate are you to have a baby?*

Not as desperate as she'd thought, she realized. Not tonight, anyway. "Actually, I'm waiting for someone," she said stiffly. "Thanks, anyway."

His eyes narrowed with irritation, and for a moment, she thought he was going to refuse to accept no for an answer. Then a tall redhead walked in wearing a skirt that could only generously be called a mini. Just that easily, he lost interest in Rachel and moved to intercept the other woman.

Shaken, Rachel gave serious consideration to walking out then and there. But she'd known this wasn't going to be easy. One of the disadvantages of looking for a father for her baby in a bar was that she would have to deal with bar flies who thought they were modern-day Casanovas. Okay, she'd dealt with her first one. She could do this.

Drawing in a calming breath, she ordered a Coke from the bartender, then waited to see which man in the crowded bar would step forward next. The place was packed with people in the medical field—she caught bits and snippets of conversation all around her about patients and surgeries and long hours of work and study. She tried to take comfort in the fact that she was in the right place. Surely somewhere in the happy-hour crowd had to be a decent man. The trick was finding him.

Later, she couldn't have said how many men approached her over the course of the next hour. It seemed like dozens, though in reality it couldn't have been more than seven or eight. And although most of them weren't nearly as obnoxious as the first man who'd approached her, they either drank more than she liked, weren't particularly attractive or didn't seem to be as kind and caring as she'd hoped for. Discouraged, she sent them packing one by one.

By nine-thirty, the crowd had thinned significantly. The bartender told her that the second wave came in after eleven, when there was a shift change at the six hospitals in the area, but she couldn't wait that long. She'd done nothing but sit at the bar and visit with the men who'd approached her, but she couldn't remember the last time she'd been so stressed. She was exhausted. And if tonight was any indication of things to come, finding a man to father her baby was going to be far more difficult than she'd originally anticipated. And she readily admitted she was worried.

Concerned, her stomach tied in knots, she kicked off her strappy high heels the second she got in her car and headed home barefoot. When the lights and the traffic of the city faded in her rearview mirror, she sighed in relief as she reached the deserted streets of Hunter's Ridge. She really did love living in a small town. There was no fancy mall, no movie theater, and the sidewalks were rolled up at seven every night, but every time she drove down the familiar tree-lined streets, she felt as if she was driving back in time.

Tonight was no different. As she headed down Main Street, there wasn't another soul in sight... except John Quinn, the deputy sheriff, who was making his rounds through the four-block downtown area. He grinned and nodded a greeting as she passed, then continued on his way. John was on patrol, she thought with a smile as she turned down her street. All was right with the world.

She'd left her porch light on, as well as a floor lamp in the living room, and in the darkness, her house looked warm and welcoming as she drove down the street. When she'd first moved to Hunter's Ridge after she and Jason divorced, she'd almost bought a house in one of the new subdivisions on the outskirts of town. She was starting her life over and she'd thought she wanted something fresh and new she could make completely hers. Then a house right around the corner from her grandmother's bakery came up for sale, and she'd stopped by to look at it. It was well over a hundred years old, had twelve-foot ceilings and aged plank flooring that bore the heel marks of countless generations that had come before. The kitchen was too small, the wiring needed to be updated, and there was no such thing as insulation in its walls, but the second she stepped inside, she'd fallen in love. She'd bought it on the spot.

The kitchen was still too small and keeping the place warm in the winter was no easy task, but given the chance, she would have bought it again in a heartbeat. Her only complaint was that the house next door was a rental that had not only fallen into disrepair but had been empty for more than a year. The owner had put it up for sale months ago, but as far as she knew, no one had even looked at the place.

As she pulled into her driveway, her headlights swept across the face of the house next door, and she hit her brakes in surprise at the sight of the lights blazing in the naked windows. Someone had moved in? When? She hadn't even realized it had been sold.

Curious, she grabbed her high-heeled sandals and stepped out of the car, her eyes trained on the long windows of the Victorian house next door. There wasn't a curtain or blind in sight, and standing in the darkness, she could easily see a man working in the living room. He was tall, but his back was to her as he tore Sheetrock off the walls. Covered in dust, his head covered with a ball cap, he could have been anywhere from thirty to a hundred and five.

If it hadn't been nearly ten o'clock at night, she would have knocked on his door and welcomed him to the neighborhood. But he was busy and it was late—her grandmother would be calling any second.

The thought had hardly registered when her cell phone rang. The new neighbor forgotten, she reached for her phone as she unlocked her front door. "Hi, Gran," she said in amusement. "I'm safe at home. You can stop worrying."

"No, I can't!" Evelyn Martin retorted. "I've been a nervous wreck all evening. So tell me everything. Are you okay? Tell me you didn't do anything!"

"I'm fine," she assured her. "Really."

"Fine, my eye," her grandmother retorted. "If you were fine, you never would have come up with this harebrained idea. I should have called your mother."

Alarmed, she warned, "Gran, you promised!"

"I know, but I'm worried, darn it! I'm afraid some creep is going to hurt you or kill you and give you some awful disease. And then what? How am I going to explain that to your mother? She never liked me, you know. She'll blame me, and then Ted will have to side with her and I'll never see him again."

Sinking down into her favorite easy chair, Rachel fought a smile. "Mom would never try to come between you and Dad. You know that. And I don't know why you think she doesn't like you. She really respects you a great deal. You started your own business when most women didn't even know how to balance a checkbook."

"I had to. We would have lost everything after Clarence died if I hadn't gone to work. And Ted would have had to go live with Clarence's aunt Myrtle, and he would have hated that. The woman starched her underwear, for heaven's sake, and smoked cigars!"

Rachel grinned. "I hate that I never met her. She sounds like a real character. A lot like you, Gran."

"I don't starch my underwear."

She chuckled at her grandmother's indignant tone, then sobered. "No, but you do your own thing. And that's what I'm doing. If I'd thought you were going to go tattling to Mom, I never would have told you my plans. You promised, Gran."

Evelyn Martin was big on promises, and they both knew it. "Okay," she huffed, "I won't tell her. It's your story to tell, not mine. But I still think you shouldn't rush into this. There are a lot of nice men out there. In fact, there's someone I want you to meet...."

"Oh, no, you don't," Rachel said quickly. "You're not setting me up again. Remember what happened the last time you tried that? He was a kid, Gran. Barely twenty-two! I felt like his mother!"

Far from apologetic, Evelyn laughed gaily. "There's nothing wrong with younger men, sweetie. Your grandfather was three years younger than me."

"Three I could handle. We're talking *thirteen,* Gran! He still lived with his parents."

"Get them young, you can raise them up the way you want," she retorted, only to laugh when Rachel just huffed in frustration. "Okay, okay, so he was a little young. This one's not. I think he's around your age. You'll like him. He's cute and clever. If he was a little older, I'd go after him myself."

"Gran!"

"Well, it's true. Always appreciate a good man, Rachel, regardless of their age."

"I do," she replied. "They're just few and far between."

"Actually, they're more common than you think," her grandmother told her. "You just can't see them because of Jason. And who can blame you? What that man did to you was criminal! He lied to you for seven years. No one in their right mind would blame you for hating his guts. Just don't paint all men with the same brush, sweetheart. Give them a chance."

"I do give them a chance."

"Yeah, right," Evelyn laughed. "Sweetie, I've seen you whenever a customer gets a little friendly. You've got No Trespassing signs posted all over you."

"I do not!"

"Remember that in the morning when Robert shows up at the bakery."

"What? *In the morning?* C'mon, Gran, give me a little time to at least prepare myself."

"You'll do fine," her grandmother assured her. "Just be nice. He's a lovely boy. You'll like him. Now, go to bed, sweetheart. You've got to look your best in the morning. Call me after you meet him."

"But—"

The line went dead, leaving her sputtering. With a groan of frustration, she shut her cell phone with a click and didn't know if she wanted to laugh or cry. Dammit, she should have seen this coming. When she'd told her grandmother her plan to find a nice medical student to father a baby for her, Evelyn had been nothing but supportive. That only should have been enough to set off Rachel's alarm bells. Her grandmother might be eccentric and outrageous at times, but when it came to family, she was a strict traditionalist. She believed in love and marriage, *then* babies.

Which was why Rachel had been so surprised when her grandmother hadn't given her much grief over her plan to have a baby. She should have known better, she thought wryly. The only reason

Evelyn had gone along with her was because, no doubt, she planned to introduce her to every known bachelor within a hundred miles of Hunter's Ridge *before* she had a chance to get pregnant. And all Rachel could do was grin and bear it. Her grandmother loved her—she just wanted the best for her. How could Rachel fault her for that?

She would, she promised herself, be nice tomorrow morning when Robert, the *lovely boy* Evelyn wanted her to meet, put in an appearance. Then she would make it very clear to him that as much as she appreciated him humoring her grandmother, she was currently taking a break from the dating scene. If he was as nice as Evelyn claimed, he would wish her luck, have coffee and a Danish on her, then be on his way with her grandmother being none the wiser.

Pleased that she would be ready for the charm of the unknown Robert, she stripped off her dating finery, took a quick shower to wash off the smell of cigarette smoke that clung to her from the bar, then fell into bed with a tired sigh. It was going on eleven—she should have been in bed two hours ago. She was exhausted, and her eyes drifted shut before her head ever hit the pillow.

Next door, the lights from her new neighbor glowed in the darkness, and the sound of someone hammering floated on the night air. Already dreaming, Rachel never noticed.

* * *

The alarm went off at the ungodly hour of four in the morning. Already awake, Rachel hit the off button and rolled out of bed. She'd always been a morning person, but adjusting to the early hours of a baker had been difficult, even for her. When she'd first moved to Hunter's Ridge to take over the bakery for her grandmother, she'd fallen asleep over dinner every night for the first three months. She was better now—she could occasionally stay up as late as eleven, but she'd learned early on that she had to hit the ground running when the alarm went off in the morning, or she'd sleep right through the breakfast rush.

In the kitchen, her coffeemaker clicked on. By the time the smell of brewing coffee drifted through the house, she was dressed and fighting with her hair. Wild and untamed, it had to be pulled back into a loose ponytail, then braided. After that, all she needed was mascara and a little lip gloss and she was ready. Taking time only to fill her travel mug with coffee, she headed for work.

She loved the morning, loved walking to work, regardless of the weather. She wouldn't have risked being out on the streets at that hour of the morning in Austin or any other major city in the country, but Hunter's Ridge was different. The last major crime wave to hit the town was three years ago, when a group of high school boys soaped the car windows of the high school principal and a dozen or so unpopular teachers. And yes, there was an occasional burglary, though those were few and far between. Most people didn't feel the need to lock their cars at night, and some didn't even lock their front doors. Rachel couldn't think of a safer place in the country to live…or raise children.

That thought brought her back to her quest for a sperm donor—and her grandmother's determination to find her a good man to marry instead. Did the unknown Robert know what her grandmother was planning for him? It didn't matter. She wasn't looking for a husband, or even someone to fall in love with. Robert, regardless of how nice he was, would have to be sent packing.

She wouldn't be rude, she assured herself as she reached the bakery and unlocked the front door. She'd just be…reserved. And busy, of course, she silently added as she flipped on lights, then hurried to the back to get started on the day's baking. After all, the mornings were the busiest time of the day for her. She was a baker, for heaven's sake! Surely the man would realize that she didn't have time to sit around and visit.

The rest of the morning crew arrived then— Sissy, Mick and Jenny—and for the next hour and a half, she had no time to even think about the unknown Robert and her grandmother's plans to find her a man. There were fresh doughnuts to make and glaze, not to mention the pastries, bread and muffins the bakery was famous for. Up to her elbows in flour, Rachel was in her element.

As a child, she'd loved visiting her grandmother, standing on a chair at her side in the bakery kitchen, learning the ins and outs of how to make a piecrust that was flaky and tender and melted in your mouth. She'd made her first pie when she was six, using a recipe that had been handed down from mother to daughter to granddaughter for generations in her grandmother's family.

If things turned out the way she hoped, she thought with a wistful smile, one day she'd have the opportunity to continue that same tradition with her own daughter.

She could just see her now, her dark curls tumbling down her back, an apron that was too big for her tied around her tiny waist as she stood next to her, rolling out the dough with fierce concentration. She'd have dimples…and blue eyes that danced with mischief and merriment….

Caught up in the fantasy, Rachel couldn't have lost track of time even if she'd wanted to. It was barely six, and her first customers of the day were waiting out on the bakery's old-fashioned porch for her to open for business. Promptly at six, she unlocked the front door and welcomed them in. Then the madness began.

She loved waiting on her customers, loved

greeting them by name and sharing part of the morning with them. She knew their likes and dislikes, who was on a diet and who wasn't, who liked soda instead of coffee, who had to rush to work, and who could sit at one of the sidewalk tables on the front porch and watch Main Street slowly come awake.

"Good morning, John. A dozen chocolate-covered doughnuts this morning?" she asked the deputy sheriff, who came in every morning to buy doughnuts for the sheriff's department. "How about a cup of coffee to go?"

His weathered face folded into a broad grin. "You know me too well, Rachel. Better add a dozen glazed, too. It's a two-doughnut day."

"You got it," she chuckled, and boxed up his order for him.

Thirty minutes after she opened the bakery for business, all the tables were full, and there was a line of customers out the door. Delighted, Rachel laughed and joked and completely forgot about the new man her grandmother had arranged for her to meet. Then suddenly, a stranger stepped up to counter and she knew this had to be Robert.

Surprised, she couldn't have said what she'd been expecting, but it wasn't the man standing in front of her. He was tall and lean, with a rugged face and the bluest eyes she'd ever seen. After Jason's betrayal, she'd been convinced that there wasn't a

man on earth who would ever get her attention
again. But one look at Robert, and her heart lurched
in her breast.

Shocked, irritated, she almost asked Sissy to wait
on him, but her pride wouldn't let her do that.
Thankful he couldn't hear the pounding of her heart,
she forced a smile. "Hi. Gran said you'd be coming
in this morning. You're a sweetheart to humor her,
but I'm not really interested. It's nothing personal,"
she added quickly when he lifted a dark brow in
surprise. "I'm just not looking for a man right now.
How about a pastry instead? Take your pick. It's my
treat. Okay?"

Chapter 2

Turk Garrison liked to think he was a man who could think fast on his feet. And it didn't take an Einstein to know that the counter woman who had just dismissed him so pleasantly obviously had mistaken him for someone else. He should have told her he wasn't who she thought he was, buy the doughnut and coffee he'd come in for, then be on his way. But there were some situations a man just couldn't walk away from, and this was one of them.

Pressing his hand to his heart, he gave her a wounded look. "I don't understand. How can you not be interested? I'm not bad-looking, everyone tells me I'm a lot of fun, and I don't pick my teeth. C'mon. Give me a chance."

Every customer in the place was listening, and more than a few were having a hard time holding back smiles. That only encouraged him more. "Ask anybody here," he told her. "They'll tell you the same thing. We could be perfect for each other, but you're not even giving me the time of day. Are you sure you want to do that? You could be turning down Mr. Wonderful."

"That's right, Rachel," an older, bald gentleman seated at a nearby table said with twinkling eyes. "At least talk to the man."

So her name was Rachel. And she blushed beautifully. She was starting to look more than a little trapped, and Turk knew he'd taken the joke far enough. "It's okay," he said, grinning. "I'm not him."

Confused, she frowned. "What?"

"You've got me confused with someone else. I don't even know your grandmother."

For a moment, she just stood there. Then he watched mortification flare in her pretty blue eyes. "Oh, God! You're not Robert? I'm so sorry! I thought—"

"No problem," he said easily. "I don't know who Robert is, but I'm glad I'm not him. So when are we going out? I've got tickets to the Stones concert Saturday night. Say the word and I'll pick you up at six…I just need your address."

He gave her a boyish grin that he had, no doubt, been flashing at females since the first one cooed at him in his mother's arms. And Rachel had to admit that it was damned effective. Dazed, she couldn't take her eyes from the crooked, enticing curve of his sensuous mouth.

Hello? Anybody home? Have you lost your mind? You're staring at the man like he just hung the moon!

The irritating little voice that whispered in her head got through to her as nothing else could. Swallowing a curse, she stiffened. What the heck was wrong with her? She didn't do this, didn't drool over a man as if she'd never seen one before... especially after the way Jason had betrayed her. The only man she wanted was a stranger she could walk away from after a one-night stand. If this man lived in Hunter's Ridge, he wouldn't be a stranger long, and she only had to see the mischief dancing in his eyes to know he wasn't the kind a woman walked away from easily. The charmers never were.

"Sorry," she retorted coolly. "I'm busy Saturday night. I have to do my laundry."

She could have done her laundry any time and the glint in his eye told her he knew it. But he accepted the excuse with a shrug and a grin. "Shot down again. Damn, I hate it when that happens. But that's okay. I'll just have to ask again when you're not so busy. See you around, sweetcakes."

Flashing his dimples at her, he stuffed a tip in the

tip jar, grabbed his coffee and the doughnut she'd sacked for him, and walked out with an easy animal grace that Rachel couldn't help but appreciate. She wasn't the only one. When she finally blinked back to attention, every other woman in the bakery was watching the long, tall drink of water saunter out of the bakery.

"I'll have some of that," Dixie Hicks sighed dreamily from a nearby table. "He's cute."

Next in line at the counter, Hilda Stevens cackled, "He certainly is. Reminds me of my third husband. I never should have let him go—he was a fantastic lover."

Three years past eighty and showing no signs of slowing down, Hilda loved nothing more than talking about her ex-husbands…and shocking people. Amused, Rachel just rolled her eyes. "Now, Hilda, you know I can't let you talk about the exes. We've got schoolkids here…."

"Oh, they're trying to decide what doughnuts they want," she scoffed. "They're not paying any attention to an old woman."

"Kids hear everything, Hilda. You know that."

"They're not going to hear the good stuff. Anyway, this is about you, not me. Why didn't you take that boy up on his invitation? *I'm not interested,*" she mimicked, scowling. "Of course you're interested! He was cute as a button. Maybe you're working too hard. I think I need to talk to your grandmother."

"No!" She was already getting enough grief from her grandmother—she didn't need more! "I appreciate your concern, Hilda, but I don't need help from Gran or anyone else. I can get my own dates."

"I wouldn't be so sure of that," the older woman retorted. "Look what you just let walk out the door!"

It had been a long time since a woman had turned him down for a date, Turk Garrison thought with a grin as he headed back to his house. His timing must have been off. That was okay—he'd ask her again. He knew where she worked. Even if he hadn't, he could walk the length and breadth of Hunter's Ridge in less than an hour. Finding her again wouldn't be a problem.

And that's what he loved about Hunter's Ridge... its size. He'd grown up in Dallas, in the shadow of his father, who was one of the most well-known heart surgeons in the city, and all he'd ever wanted to be was a small-town doctor like his grandfather. For his father's sake, however, he'd tried to follow in his footsteps, but he'd hated it. He'd given it two years—that was all he could manage. Now he was going to do what he wanted to do.

Have you lost your mind? What kind of career can you have in a small town? There's no future there. No money! You've got the hands of a heart surgeon. It's in your blood! You can't walk away from that to play Marcus Welby in Small Town, America! It's insane.

His father had never been one to pull his punches, and he certainly hadn't when he'd informed him last month that he intended to resign from his father's practice and open his own clinic in Hunter's Ridge. He'd ranted and raved and tried to reason with him, and when that hadn't worked, he'd used his most powerful weapon—Janice, Turk's mother.

To her credit, his mother had sympathized with his dream of having a less-complicated life and practice. But ultimately, she, too, had stressed how much he would be giving up if he chose Hunter's Ridge over Dallas…wealth, prestige, professional affiliations with some of the top surgeons in the country. How could he give that up? Why would he want to?

Watching a family of ducks walk across River Road to the river, Turk would never understand how his parents understood him so little. There was no question that his father was successful when it came to making money—but he often passed patients on the street and didn't have a clue who they were. Turk's grandfather, on the other hand, not only knew his patients, he knew their children, their hopes and fears, their birthdays and anniversaries and where they planned to be buried.

That was what Turk wanted, what he intended to have.

Even though he'd told his parents he was settling in Hunter's Ridge, they hadn't really believed he'd leave Dallas and turn his back on the kind of career he could have there. That, however, is exactly what he'd done. He'd found office space in the town's newest—and only—strip mall, spent the last two weeks hiring staff and advertising the fact that Hunter's Ridge had a new doctor in town. The clinic opened for business tomorrow, and it was only three blocks from his house. He'd be able to walk to work every day.

"You're not in Dallas anymore, Doc," he told himself with a grin. And that was never more apparent than when he strolled up the front walk to his house.

There was no doubt that it was a fixer-upper. A block off Main Street, it was a hundred years old and looked it. It hadn't been painted in years, the gutters were drooping, and there was more than one rotting eave that needed to be replaced. The wiring was iffy, the plumbing hadn't been updated in fifty years, and the pier-and-beam foundation obviously needed some major adjustments—windows and doors throughout the house didn't shut properly. But the place had good bones. It had ten-foot ceilings, crown molding and stained glass, and it reminded him of his grandparents' house. He'd taken one look at it and bought it on the spot.

His friends and family thought he was crazy, but he was doing much of the work himself. He enjoyed the physical labor and liked the idea of putting his own stamp on the place. He'd been tearing out

Sheetrock almost from the moment he'd moved in two days ago. Once he had it all out, he'd have to bring in an electrician and plumber and a foundation repairman, but in the meantime, he was having a hell of a good time.

Unlocking the front door, he stepped inside and grinned. His mother would have had a stroke if she could see the way he was living. It would be months before the house was no longer a construction zone, so he'd placed all his furniture in storage, then bought a few secondhand pieces to use in the house during the remodeling. He had an old wooden straight chair and a TV tray that he used in the kitchen, a scarred bed and dresser in the huge master bedroom, and an ancient recliner in the living room. And everywhere he looked, there was a fine coating of Sheetrock dust. And he'd just started tearing it out. He could just imagine what the place was going to look like in a few weeks.

From the backyard, Daisy, his yellow Lab, knew the instant he walked into the kitchen. She gave a sharp bark at the back door, but he only laughed. "Oh, no, you don't," he called through the door. "I want to work on the Sheetrock, and if I let you in, I won't get a thing done. Wait a second. I've got a treat for you."

He found a steak bone in the refrigerator from last night's dinner and opened the back door to offer it to Daisy. She wasn't a pig when it came to snacks—taking the bone very delicately, she turned and trotted into her doghouse. Turk knew she wouldn't come out again until the bone was history. Grinning, he grabbed his hammer and nail puller and went to work.

Five hours later, he had a mess on his hands. The floor in the master bedroom was a foot deep with broken pieces of Sheetrock and enough dust to choke a horse. And that was just from the demolition of one wall. Pleased, he attacked the debris on the floor with a commercial broom and dustpan, then spent the next thirty minutes carting it all out to the Dumpster. When he finished, one wall was bare of Sheetrock, and the floor was broom-clean.

Planning to start on the west wall of the bedroom next, he'd just walked into the kitchen to see about making a sandwich for a late lunch when he heard Daisy barking angrily in the backyard. Surprised— she was usually pretty mild-mannered—he glanced out the kitchen window just in time to see her chase a cat across the backyard. A split second later, the cat—and Daisy—sailed over the back fence without ever breaking stride.

"What the hell!" Jerking open the back door, he yelled "Daisy! Get your butt back in this yard right this minute!"

He might as well have told the wind not to blow. Daisy never looked back.

"Damn!" Swearing, he took off after her.

Later, he couldn't have said how many streets he ran down, how many times he came so close to catching her that he could see the mischief dancing in her eyes. Then she would take off again, barking in excitement at the game. Huffing and puffing, he had no choice but to follow. Hunter's Ridge had a leash law, but that was the least of his worries. He loved the goofball and it'd break his heart if she darted into the road and got hit.

Ten minutes later, he came around a corner and spied her standing in the front yard of a house that was very much like his, but beautifully restored. At first, he thought Daisy had mistaken the place for home...then, as he drew closer, he realized that she was too busy eating something to notice the house—or the fact that he was quickly bearing down on her.

Relieved, he grabbed her collar. "Gotcha!" Only then did he realize that she hadn't dug up a bone somewhere. She was eating a cherry pie!

"Daisy! Oh, my God! Where'd you get that?"

Glancing sharply around, he spied a table on the side porch of the house they stood right in front of. There were two other pies cooling there. Swearing, he gave Daisy a reproving look. "Shame on you! This isn't the way to meet the neighbors! Or potential patients! Now what are we going to do?"

Totally unconcerned, Daisy licked her chops as she finished the rest of her pie.

"C'mon," Turk growled, tightening his grip on her collar. "It's time to fess up."

Bracing for a tongue-lashing—Daisy hadn't just snatched any pie; it was a homemade one!—he knocked on the door, then waited. Through the frosted oval glass of the front door, Turk could just make out the blurred figure of a woman approaching. "Wipe that smile off your face," he told Daisy quickly. "At least try to look contrite."

The words were hardly out of his mouth when the door was pulled open and he found himself facing an older, white-haired woman with rounded cheeks, a quick smile and faded blue eyes that seemed to have a perpetual twinkle.

Her gaze moving from him to Daisy and back again, she lifted a delicately arched brow. "Yes? May I help you?"

"I'm sorry, ma'am," he said with a rueful smile, "but I seem to owe you an apology."

Surprised, she blinked. "I don't think so, young man. I don't even know you."

"I just moved to town this week," he explained, and held out his hand. "I'm Turk Garrison. And this is Daisy," he added, nodding to the Lab. "She owes you an apology, too. She just ate one of your pies."

"What?" Startled, she glanced past him to the side porch, where an empty trivet spoke of the missing pie.

Watching the emotions flicker lightning quick

across her face, Turk wouldn't have blamed her if she'd given him a piece of her mind. Daisy had wolfed down in seconds something that had, no doubt, taken her hours to make. She had every right to be furious.

Instead, she laughed. "Well, this is a first."

"I'm so sorry."

"It wasn't your fault," she assured him. "Or Daisy's." Holding out her hand to the dog so she could sniff it, she grinned when Daisy licked her fingers. "I was the one who put the pies outside," she told Turk, her blue eyes twinkling behind the lenses of her wire-rimmed glasses. "And I'll tell right now, they smelled darn good. How was a dog supposed to resist?"

"But—"

"It was just a pie. No harm done. I can make another one." The matter settled, she held out her hand. "I'm Evelyn Martin. Welcome to Hunter's Ridge. How about a piece of pie for you? I just finished lunch and was about to have some dessert and coffee. We can have it out here on the porch and you can tell me all about yourself. Are you married? I've got a granddaughter…"

"Oh, no," he said quickly, laughing. "Nothing against your granddaughter, but I just moved away from my woman problems. I don't need any more. Not that your granddaughter would be a problem," he quickly assured her. "I'm sure she's very nice, but—"

"It's okay," she chuckled. "I'm not offended. You'll change your mind if you ever meet her. In the meantime, you should know I make a darn good pie—best in the county. If you don't believe me, ask Daisy."

Daisy barked at the mention of her name, drawing a laugh from both of them. "I'm sure it was delicious," Turk said wryly. "I've never seen her gulp down anything like she did that pie, but I've really got to get home. Thanks again, though, for being so understanding. Daisy and I owe you."

"No problem," she replied. "I'm sure I'll see you around town. And come back when you've got some time. We'll talk."

Promising to do just that, Turk headed home with Daisy in tow, thankful that the two of them had gotten off so lightly. "You're just darn lucky that Mrs. Martin didn't call the dog catcher on you," he told the Lab as they reached the house. "You could be at the pound right now and I'd be fined for disobeying the leash law."

Far from chastised, Daisy just wandered over to her bed in the corner of the living room and collapsed with a heartfelt sigh. Within a matter of moments, she was snoring.

Turk rolled his eyes. "Brat. You've got your belly full of cherry pie and now it's time for a nap. You don't have to worry about anybody wanting to set you up with some cute chick. No, I'm the lucky one who gets to deal with that. Twice in one day. That's got to be some kind of record. It must be something in the water here."

It was more than that, however, and he knew it. Women just liked to set people up, and now that he was the new man in town, he's was probably going to get hit a lot with that. And he could handle it, he assured himself. After dealing with Susan and Laureen, he could deal with just about anything.

He still didn't know how he'd gotten himself into such a mess. Susan Presley was the daughter of his father's best friend, and she and Turk had lived together for the past year and a half. He'd thought she was the woman he was going to spend the rest of his life with. Then he'd told her he was going to give up working with his father to move to Hunter's Ridge, and she'd dropped him like a hot rock.

He was stunned and hurt. Then his friends had convinced him the only way to get over one woman was to go out with another. So he'd asked Laureen Becker out. A nurse at the hospital, she was cute and fun and didn't appear to be the gold digger that Susan was. Then a week after they'd gone out a couple of times, she'd told everyone at the hospital that they were engaged.

Turk's gut knotted just at the thought of how Laureen had reacted when he questioned her about the rumor. Not that least bit chagrined that he'd found out about the rumor and that she was the one spreading it, she only smiled and kissed him and told him of course they were getting married. She wasn't like Susan. She knew a good man when she saw one and she'd fallen in love with him the first time she laid eyes on him. She knew he felt the same way.

He'd thought she was joking. They'd only gone out twice! And he hadn't done anything more than kiss her, and his heart hadn't been in that. He couldn't tell her that, of course—he wasn't that insensitive. So he'd tried to spare her feelings and explained instead that he was moving, starting a new life, and he was doing that alone. Any woman with an ounce of pride would have assured him she was just teasing and let the subject pass. Not Laureen. Far from discouraged, she'd laughed...then assured him that he would eventually realize they were soulmates. He just needed time.

She'd been so confident, she'd scared the hell out of him. Left with no choice but to be brutally honest, he'd made it clear that not only were they *not* soulmates, he didn't love her, she wasn't a part of his future, and she never would be. Then he'd broken things off with her and hadn't spoken to her since.

That was a month ago. Considering how determined she'd seemed, he hadn't expected her to let him walk away without a fight. But that's exactly what she'd done. There'd been no phone calls, no letters, no more rumors that they were engaged. She'd avoided him like the plague, thank God, and he'd left Dallas without contacting her again. It was over.

Then, she'd left a message on his cell phone yesterday morning. And last night. And both messages were virtually the same.

"Turk, sweetheart, how are you? I know you must be incredibly busy, setting up your practice and everything, darling, but I thought you'd call me by now. Do you miss me? I think of you constantly. I know you must do the same. Isn't it awful? We have to find a way to be together, darling. Have you found us a house yet? When you do, let me know. I can decorate it for us. We're going to have a wonderful home, sweetheart. Think of that, think of me, in the dark of night, when you're all alone and missing me. We'll be together soon, darling. I promise. Then we'll never have to be apart again. I love you. I don't need to tell you that—you already know. Call me when you can."

He should have called her and made it clear once and for all that she was wasting her time—he wanted nothing to do with her. But there was something in her voice that turned his blood to ice. Something that set alarm bells clanging in his head. Something that wasn't quite right. And for the life of him, he couldn't put his finger on what it was…confidence, determination, insanity. Whatever it was, he knew he wanted nothing to do with it…or her. Immediately calling his cell phone company, he changed his cell phone number.

Chapter 3

Turk readily admitted he wasn't much of a cook—
he'd never had time to develop that particular skill.
But how difficult could it be? All he had to do was
follow the directions on the box. So with a great
deal of confidence, he turned on the oven, slid the
frozen cherry pie he'd bought at the store onto the
center rack, then set the timer on the stove. Now all
he had to do was wait. Piece of cake.

Lying in the kitchen doorway, Daisy watched his
every move with sparkling brown eyes that missed
little. "Don't even think of going there," Turk
warned her. "You've already had one pie today—

you're not getting another. This one's for Mrs. Martin. We owe her."

Resigned, Daisy laid her chin on her paws and gave a heavy sigh.

Amused, Turk added, "And you're not going with me to deliver it. So if you think you can con her out of a piece, forget it. You're grounded. Remember? You're not going anywhere until you learn how to behave in public."

He didn't doubt that Daisy understood every word—her brown eyes twinkled at the challenge—but she only shifted, as if to shrug, and closed her eyes. Satisfied she wasn't going anywhere, he strode into the living room to start working on the Sheetrock again.

Caught up in his work, he didn't, at first, hear the timer go off in the kitchen. Then he smelled the pie. It smelled...slightly burnt.

"Damn!" Lightning quick, he raced into the kitchen and jerked open the oven door. One look at the darkened edges of the crust and he started to swear. Daisy barked in total agreement. "I know, I know," he grumbled. "You don't have to tell me— I can see it's a little too brown. What the hell happened? I followed the directions!"

He started to reach for the pie, only to re- member to grab a hot pad at the last minute. Setting the darn thing on top of the stove to cool, he turned off the oven, then surveyed the pie with a frown. "Maybe it's not so bad," he told Daisy, not sure if he was trying to convince her or himself. "The middle looks okay. And it's really not burned, just a little too brown. Most people don't eat the crust anyway, and I don't have another one. It's the thought that counts, anyway. We—" he gave the dog a baleful look "—took a pie, so we're returning one. I'm sure Mrs. Martin will appreciate that, especially since I've never baked anything before."

She would, no doubt, laugh at his poor attempt at baking, but Turk couldn't blame her for that. He was sure it didn't measure up to her homemade masterpiece, but it really wasn't that bad for a first effort and it smelled great. If the situation were reversed, he'd laugh, himself. It was just about the worst pie he'd ever seen. Given the chance, Daisy would have eaten it in a heartbeat.

Reading his mind, the dog moaned pitifully. Laughing, Turk set the pie on top of the refrigerator to cool. "Don't even think about it," he warned Daisy when she looked around for the closest chair. "You're already grounded. Don't make it worse for yourself."

For an answer, Daisy plopped down onto the floor in front of the fridge.

Leaving her on guard duty—and knowing she couldn't reach the pie regardless of how she tried— Turk headed down the hall to the bathroom to wash off the Sheetrock dust that seemed to cover him from head to toe. Fifteen minutes later, it was time to face the music.

Daisy was right where he'd left her, and the second he reached for the pie, she jumped up, tail wagging furiously, and barked in excitement. "Sorry, Daisy," he retorted with a grin. "You're still grounded. I'll be back in fifteen minutes. Try to behave yourself while I'm gone."

She was still barking at him as he strode out the front door.

He made the walk to Evelyn Martin's in less than ten minutes. Striding down her front walk, he considered leaving the pie on the table on the side porch, but it was already almost dark and she probably wouldn't see it until morning. She didn't, in fact, appear to even be home. The house was dark, the front shades drawn.

Frowning—he refused to take the pie back to Daisy!—he knocked sharply at the front door, and only then realized that there was a light shining at the back of the house in what was, probably, the kitchen. Through the cut-glass window of the front door, he could just make out the shadowy image of a woman walking toward him.

Good. She was home, he thought with a grin. He didn't doubt for a minute that she'd chew him out for going to so much trouble, but if she was anything like his own grandmother, she wouldn't turn down the pie…even if it was store-bought.

"I hope you don't mind me showing up on your

doorstep again—" Whatever he was going to say next flew right out of his head at the sight of the woman who opened the door to him. Instead of Evelyn Martin, he found himself face-to-face with the sassy woman who'd waited on him at the bakery that morning. The same woman who'd thought he'd been sent there by her grandmother.

A grin tugging at his lips, he drawled, "Well, if it isn't the doughnut lady. What brings you here, sweetcakes?"

Caught off guard, Rachel blinked, her heart jumping in her breast at the sight of wicked blue eyes that looked vaguely familiar. Where had she seen those eyes before? And that smile…crooked, mischievous, flirty. Then it hit her. The man in the bakery that morning! The one she'd mistakenly thought her grandmother had tried to set her up with!

"Aha," he drawled, watching recognition flicker in her eyes. "You remember. I knew you would. I'm the kind of man a woman can't forget."

It was an outrageous claim…accompanied by a wink and a grin that were impossible to ignore. Damn the man, why did he have to be so charming? "I can't argue with that," she retorted. "A woman always remembers the—"

"Now, now, don't be nasty," he cut in quickly, recognizing a good-natured insult when he saw it coming. "You know you're charmed. Go ahead. Admit it. I dare you."

Her lips twitched and there wasn't a damn thing she could do about it. Even when she scowled, she found herself fighting a smile. "I don't take dares."

"Ah…there's your problem," he said with twinkling eyes. "Life's too short to always play it safe. You should live a little—"

"Rachel? Who's at the door?" Evelyn Martin suddenly called from the kitchen.

"It's all right, Gran," she said quickly.

"Who are you talking to?" Stepping from the kitchen, Evelyn joined her, only to smile with delight at the sight of the visitor standing at the front door. "Turk! How nice to see you again! Come in. Rachel, invite the man in, for heaven's sake, sweetheart."

Surprised, Rachel blinked. "You two know each other?"

"My dog…*borrowed*…one of your grandmother's pies this afternoon," Turk replied. "I'm returning it."

"Oh, how nice of you!" Evelyn said, delighted. "But you didn't have to go to all that trouble."

"I owed you," he said simply, holding it out to her. "It's a little brown around the edges—I never made a pie before. And it's just one of those frozen ones from the grocery store—"

"It looks great," she assured him, eagerly taking it and completely overlooking the edges of the crust. "Have you had supper? Rachel and I were just about to sit down to eat. Oh, my goodness, where are my manners? You haven't met my granddaughter, have you? Rachel, this is Turk Garrison. We met this afternoon when he was nice enough to knock on the door and tell on his dog."

"I had to," Turk retorted. "She's a thief, pure and simple, and she didn't show an ounce of remorse when I grounded her and restricted her to the house. That must have been one heck of a pie."

Evelyn chuckled. "Poor baby. I'll make her a pie when she's off restriction—something with meat. She'll love it."

"Lucky dog," Turk grumbled, grinning. "Tell me the next time you're going to set a pie out to cool and I'll make sure to steal one."

"You don't have to go that far," Evelyn told him with twinkling eyes. "I just pulled a chicken pot pie from the oven—it's Rachel's favorite. I'm sure she wouldn't mind if you stayed and joined us for dinner. And we'll have your pie for dessert."

The words were hardly out of her mouth when Rachel spoke up quickly. "He probably has other plans, Gran."

"Actually, I don't," he said easily, and grinned when she shot him a narrow-eyed look of pure female irritation. "I'd love to stay…if that's all right with you."

She was fuming, but to her credit, she didn't blast him like she so obviously wanted to. "Of course it's all right," she said, giving him a tight smile. "I'll set another plate at the table."

When she whirled and headed for the kitchen, her grandmother chuckled, her blue eyes dancing with anticipation. "This is going to be fun. C'mon in."

Later, Turk had to admit that the chicken pot pie was the best he'd ever eaten. It was the conversation, however, that made the meal. He'd hardly sat down at Evelyn Martin's round, antique oak table in her dining room when she began to sing Rachel's praises. "She's my favorite granddaughter."

"I'm your only granddaughter," Rachel said dryly. "I'm sure Mr. Garrison would rather talk about something else—"

"It's Turk," he cut in with a wink. "And the topic of conversation is just fine. Did you grow up in Hunter's Ridge? You don't have much of a Texas accent."

"She grew up in Colorado," her grandmother supplied when Rachel just frowned at him. "She moved to Hunter's Ridge five years ago to help me in the bakery. I retired last summer and she's been running the place ever since. She does a good job, doesn't she?"

"Gran!"

Grinning, Turk nodded. "Best doughnuts I ever ate. Your recipe?"

"It was...until Rachel decided to change it a

little. In fact, she's put her stamp on everything in the bakery, and it shows. I hate to admit it, but she's a better cook than I am. She's going to make some man a great wife."

For a moment, Turk thought Rachel was not only going to strangle her grandmother, but him, too. "I don't think Mr. Garrison is interested in what kind of wife I'll make," she replied, shooting her grandmother a quelling look. "You didn't invite him to dinner to talk about me—"

"Well, of course I did, sweetheart," Evelyn broke in with a wide-eyed smile. "Hunter's Ridge isn't all that big. I knew the second he knocked on my door that the two of you should meet."

"And here I am, showing up at your front door just like Mr. Right," Turk added, wicked humor dancing in his eyes. "Do you believe in fate or what?"

When Turk and her grandmother just grinned at her, she wanted to shoot them both. "No," she huffed, "I don't. And you didn't show up at my front door—only Gran's. So it looks like the two of *you* are fated to be together. Darn. And I had such high expectations."

Surprised, Turk burst out laughing. "You're good, sweetcakes! But don't forget—I did show up at your place first. The bakery," he reminded her with a quick grin before she could argue the point. "This morning? When you broke my heart and turned me down flat? I was devastated."

"Yeah, right," she snorted.

Evelyn clicked her tongue. "You have to give the man a chance, sweetie." Turning her attention back to Turk, she said, "You have to tell the girl something about yourself, Turk. You can't just expect her to realize you could be Mr. Right when she knows next to nothing about you."

"That's right," Rachel threw in. "For all I know, you could be Ted Bundy."

"Feel free to check me out," he retorted easily. "I haven't killed anyone in years."

Amused, Evelyn said, "Of course you haven't. So what do you do, Turk? If you hope to win Rachel, you've got to make a decent living, you know. She's not some sugar mama, looking for a man to support."

"Then today's her lucky day. I—"

"He's in construction!" Rachel cut in, suddenly remembering where she'd seen him before. "I thought you looked familiar when you came into the bakery this morning. You bought the house next door to me! I saw you working on it last night."

It was Turk's turn to be surprised. "You live next door?"

"You're kidding?!" Evelyn exclaimed, laughing. "You two live next door to each other? Sounds like fate to me." When Rachel sent her a warning look, she chuckled. "Sorry, sweetie. I couldn't resist. I call 'em as I see 'em."

When Rachel just snorted, Evelyn grinned and arched a brow at Turk. "So you bought the Sanderson place? It's been empty for years. I always thought that was such a shame—I remember it as a girl. It was a wonderful place. It just needs a little TLC."

"My thoughts, exactly," he replied. "I can't believe it was on the market all those years and no one snapped it up."

"Are you fixing it up to sell? You probably bought it for a song—you could make a good profit. I bet that's what you do, isn't it? Buy old houses, fix them up, then sell them for a nice profit. I've heard a lot of people are doing that."

"Me, too, but I'm not one of them. I just liked the house. Actually, I'm a doctor."

Whatever he'd been expecting, it wasn't the reaction he got. Sudden silence greeted his announcement, and Rachel couldn't have looked more stunned if he'd hit her in the head with a hammer. Her grandmother gasped softly, then looked quickly at Rachel, her dancing blue eyes alight with an interest that Turk was all too familiar with. He'd lost track over the years of the number of women who sat up and took notice when they learned he was a doctor.

Laureen had been the worst—he could have been Attila the Hun and she still would have chased him simply because of two little initials after his name. He hadn't thought Rachel was that way—mercen-

ary women didn't usually look after their grand-
mothers and give free pastries to every new
customer who walked in the door. But what, after
all, did he really know about her? Just because her
grandmother said Rachel was a soft touch and
everyone in town knew it, didn't mean that she really
was. For all he knew, she could be as merciless as
Laureen and after the money she thought he had.

Evelyn tried to hold back a smile and failed mis-
erably. "A doctor? Really? That's fascinating.
Rachel's been looking for a good doctor."

"Gran!"

At Rachel's warning tone, Turk studied the two
of them with narrowed eyes. "Why do I have the
feeling I've missed something? What's the joke?"

"Nothing," Rachel said quickly. "Gran's just
pushing my buttons. I have a…mole…in a delicate
spot, and that's all I'm going to say about it. Now,
how about some pie? I don't know about you two,
but I could use something sweet. Gran, why don't
you get the pie while I get the dessert plates?"

Not giving her grandmother a chance to bring
up her "medical" problem again, she jumped up
from the table to retrieve the dessert plates from the
china cabinet. Amused, Evelyn told Turk, "Well, I
guess we're having dessert now. Excuse me while
I get the pie."

She was back in a split second with the pie and
a fancy serving piece to cut it. Remembering the

wonderful homemade pie Daisy had gobbled up, Turk grimaced at his own offering. "I didn't realize when I decided to replace the pie that Daisy ate that you had your own bakery. If your own pies taste half as good as they look, you're not going to want to eat mine. Why don't we just say we ate it and toss it? I don't want to be accused of poisoning you, on top of everything else."

"You worry too much," Evelyn replied easily, shrugging off his concern. "It'll be fine."

But when she cut the first piece of pie and started to transfer it to a dessert plate, it became quickly apparent that the pie was anything but okay. The bottom crust was still raw.

Turk took one look at it and groaned. "I knew it! I should have just gone to your own bakery and bought you a pie."

Evelyn laughed. "Will you chill? It's just a pie and you've never baked one before. I'll just put it back in the oven and bake it a little longer. It shouldn't take longer than fifteen minutes or so."

"I'll do it," Rachel said quickly.

"That's all right, sweetie—I've got it," Evelyn assured her, and snatched up the pie before Rachel could beat her to the punch. "Why don't you and Turk get to know each other better? I'll make some coffee while the pie's baking."

Grinning, she hurried into the kitchen and never saw the flash of frustration in her granddaughter's eyes. Turk, however, did. Leaning back in his chair, he surveyed Rachel in amusement. "You know, we didn't get off to a very good start this morning. Shall we start over?"

"That's not necessary—"

"It's nice to meet you," he continued, giving her an easy smile as he extended his hand across the table to shake hers. "I'm Turk Garrison. I'm new in town and looking for someone to show me around. Wanna volunteer? I promise I don't bite, scratch or drool in public. So whaddaya say? Are you game?"

Unable to take her eyes off his engaging smile, Rachel tried hard not to be charmed. She was fighting a losing battle. She wanted to say yes so badly she could taste it. Instead, she said, "No."

Wounded, he pressed a hand to his heart. "No? What do you mean...*no?* How can you say no to this face? Are you worried I'll jump you or something? I'm harmless. Really!"

She'd never seen a less harmless man in her life. "And I'm Queen Elizabeth," she retorted. "I know a line when I hear one."

"Really? I've never been more serious in my life."

If he hadn't been so cocky, so darn sure of himself—not to mention, boyishly attractive—she might have taken him more seriously. But a woman only had to look at him to know that he was trouble any way you looked at him. And that was the last thing she wanted or needed. She just wanted a sperm donor. Under no circumstances could he be the man next door.

"I appreciate the invitation—"

"But you have to do your laundry," he finished for her, grinning. "That's okay. I can wait until you don't have an excuse. I'm a patient man. And it's not like I don't know where to find you. You're right next door."

He had her and they both knew it. Talk about dumb luck! She'd never step out her front door again without thinking of him! Her heart thumped at the thought, irritating her no end, but she just smiled sweetly at him. "Did I mention that I'm not looking for a man? How patient are you?"

"I guess we'll have to wait and see," he said with a chuckle. "This is going to be fun."

She gave him a withering look, but before she could tell him he was setting himself up for a fall, her grandmother returned with the pie Turk had brought. It was now nicely browned and bubbling. "Now we can have dessert," she said happily.

Quickly returning to the kitchen for the coffee she'd made, she took her seat and glanced back and forth between the two of them. "Well? How's it going? Are you friends yet?"

"Not exactly," Rachel said dryly.

"We were just discussing the fact that we're neighbors," Turk retorted, winking at her as he took the piece of pie she offered him. "I don't know how Rachel feels about coincidence, but I don't think there's any such thing. Everything happens for a reason."

"It's a small town," she pointed out. "You were bound to live somewhere close by."

"But next door? C'mon, Rachel, what are the odds? I'm telling you, it's fate."

"He's got a point, dear," Evelyn said with a chuckle. "Somebody upstairs obviously wanted the two of you to meet." Turning her attention back to Turk, she grinned. "So do you think you're going to like Hunter's Ridge? It's a great place to live…and raise a family. Do you want children, Turk?"

"Gran—"

At Rachel's warning tone, Evelyn told Turk, "She thinks I'm being too personal. I was just curious. So many young people today are so interested in their careers that they don't have time to have children. And since you're a doctor, your career must be very important to you…."

"It's important," he agreed, finishing the last bite of his pie, "it's just not everything. That's one of the reasons I moved to Hunter's Ridge. My grandfather was a small-town doctor, and his patients weren't just people he saw when they were sick. He was friends with everyone in town. I hope I can have the same kind of life in Hunter's Ridge."

"Oh, you can," Evelyn assured him. "We need a

good doctor. And Rachel can introduce you around…."

"I'm counting on it," he said with a grin. "Now, I really have to go, ladies. Thanks for dinner and dessert, but I've really got to be going. Next time'll be my treat."

He was gone with a wink and a grin, and Rachel told herself she was glad. If her heart was knocking against her ribs and she had a feeling she wasn't going to shake Turk Garrison nearly as easily as she'd like, she kept that to herself. Her grandmother was already far too pleased with herself, as it was.

"He's perfect for you."

Rachel rolled her eyes at her grandmother's delighted words. "No, he's not! What were you thinking…telling him I'd show him around town? He's already too cocky as it is."

"He's just pushing your buttons," her grandmother told her, chuckling. "And he's really good at it. I'm telling you…you should go after that young man. He's a doctor, for heaven's sake, and you know that's what you wanted. Someone kind and caring and intelligent. Those were your exact words."

"Yes, but—"

"And he likes children. He's charming, attractive, everything a woman could want in a husband. And he lives right next door to you! What's not to love?"

"I've had a husband, Gran," she reminded her. "I don't want another one."

"I know that, sweetheart. And I understand. What Jason did to you was outrageous, and I don't blame you for not wanting to jump back into a relationship. But Jason was the exception, not the rule. Give Turk a chance. You could do worse, sweetheart. A lot worse. He's quite charming."

When Rachel just gave her a baleful look, she laughed. "Okay, okay. I've had my say—it's your decision, your choice. I'll keep my opinion to myself."

"Yeah, right," Rachel drawled. "You couldn't keep your opinion to yourself if your life depended on it."

Her blue eyes twinkling, Evelyn didn't deny it. "Opinions are like…birthdays. Everyone's got one, but they're no fun if you don't share them."

It took all of ten minutes for Turk to walk home. As he strode up the front walk, he found his gaze drifting to the house next door. So the very cute Ms. Martin slept fifty feet away from his bedroom. Who knew? He couldn't wait to tease her about that and watch her eyes snap.

Caught up in the image, he was jerked back to his surroundings by the ringing of his cell phone. Checking the caller ID, he groaned. Another call from his mother. Irritated with him for walking away from the big-city practice that had been planned for him from the moment he'd been born, his father had washed his hands of him. His mother, on the other hand, hadn't given up nearly as easily.

She'd called him every day since he'd left and pleaded with him to reconsider his decision.

Knowing today would be no different, he was tempted not to answer. He could always claim his battery was dead and he never got the call. But guilt tugged at him and he knew he couldn't do it. So he flipped open his phone and said, "Hi, Mom. If you're calling again to try to change my mind, let's don't go there today. Okay? We've already been there, and there's no point in rehashing everything."

To her credit, she didn't cry as he'd half expected. Instead, she sighed, "If you insist. I just feel like you made a hasty decision—"

"I've been thinking about doing this since I was twelve years old, Mom. There's nothing hasty about it. I know what I want, so if that's why you called…"

"Wait! Don't hang up. I called to tell you that Becky Richards called this morning. She's moved back to Dallas and would love to see you."

If Turk hadn't been prepared for such a tactic, he would have laughed. He'd taken Becky Richards to the junior-senior prom and had only one other date with her before she dumped him for the captain of the football team. From what he remembered, they'd graduated from high school without ever going out again.

"C'mon, Mom! This is just another excuse to get me to come back to Dallas, and it's not going to work. You know I don't care about Becky Richards. That's ancient history."

"You liked her once—"

"I was sixteen! Will you stop! I'm not coming back to Dallas for Becky Richards or anyone else. This is my home now. I'm sorry you and Dad can't accept that."

"We just want what's best for you," she sniffed. "If you just weren't so stubborn!"

"I come by it honestly," he said wryly. "Look, I've got to get back to work on the house. I'll call you guys Thursday night. Okay?"

She wasn't happy about being cut off, but she grudgingly said, "Okay. Just think about what I said."

"I will," he promised. "I love you. Tell Dad I'll talk to him Thursday."

He hung up before she could think of another argument, but he'd barely clipped his phone back on his belt when it rang again. Snatching it back to his ear, he said, "You didn't have to call me back to tell me you love me. I already know that."

Expecting his mother to scold him for hanging up so abruptly, he was met with nothing but silence. Surprised, he pulled the phone away from his ear to check caller ID, and swore silently when he saw it was a private number. Without a word, he quickly hung up.

Even as his stomach knotted with tension and a voice in his head told him that Laureen had somehow gotten his new cell phone number, his common sense told him he was being paranoid. He'd given the new number to only two people—his parents. And as much as they wanted him back in Dallas, they would never give his number to anyone, especially Laureen. They didn't even know her.

He had nothing to worry about, he told himself as he shook off his troubled thoughts and went inside to change into his work clothes. Five minutes later, he was back at work, tearing out Sheetrock, and Laureen was just a distant, unpleasant memory that had no place in his new life.

Chapter 4

The next morning, Turk arrived at the bakery bright and early, only to discover ten people lined up ahead of him, waiting for the doors to open. So much for getting there first and having some time to flirt with Rachel before the rest of her customers arrived, he thought ruefully. He'd just have to do it in front of half the town.

The doors opened promptly at six, just as they had, no doubt, for the past fifty years. Across a sea of heads, Turk's eyes met Rachel's, and she immediately stiffened. Amused, he wondered if she had a clue how easy she was to tease. Before he could even say good morning, however, he was swept inside by the crowd, and almost immediately, the warm scent of yeast and baking bread and cinnamon attacked his senses. His mouth watered, his stomach grumbled, and just that quickly, she had the advantage in the little game of flirting he was waging.

"You don't fight fair," he told her when it was his time to order.

Surprised, she eyed him warily. "I have no idea what you're talking about."

"Of course you do," he quipped. "A man comes in here all prepared to flirt and tease and dazzle you with his wit, but before he can say a word, he gets a whiff of the scents floating from your kitchen, and all he can think about is his stomach. It's really quite irritating."

She didn't smile, but for a split second, he thought her lips twitched. Then she stiffened, her brows knitting in a scowl, and he almost laughed. Maybe he was getting to her, after all!

"You can stuff the flirting," she told him coolly. "The only thing that's going to get you anywhere in here is money for your order. What'll you have? Coffee and a French twist? Or something a little more adventuresome for the new doctor in town? How about a pig in a blanket?"

He grinned. "A pig in a blanket, huh? You think I don't know what that is, don't you? I'll have you know, I make them all the time."

"Oh, really? So what are they?"

"Pigs...must be pork...ham?"

"Breakfast sausage," she said dryly, "baked in a roll."

"Try them and be done with it," an older man at the end of the line growled. "If you want to flirt, do it on your own time. You're holding all these people up."

"Stop that, Stu Butler!" the gray-haired woman in front of him in line scolded. "Let the man flirt. If you'd done it more at his age, we might still be married!"

Everyone in the bakery burst into laughter, but Turk had to give the old man credit—he joined in. "You never did have any trouble telling it like it is, Ethel. Okay, I'll let the man flirt."

"Actually, I'm done," Turk chuckled. "For now. I'll just sit in the corner and eat my pigs in a blanket and watch the lady work."

In five seconds flat, Rachel had his order together. "You know, you could eat this down by the river," she said. "It's a good morning to watch the ducks."

"No, thanks," he retorted, handing her a five dollar bill. "I like the view here just fine."

Grinning, he dropped the change she returned to him in the tip jar, then moved to one of the few empty tables in the dining area. Irritated, Rachel tried to ignore him, but the man was impossible! He made no secret of the fact that he was watching her every move, and her customers loved it. Fighting grins—grinning outright, dammit!—they watched

Turk watch her and whispered among themselves, actually taking bets on how long it would take for her to come to her senses and go out with the man. And he was loving it. Every time her gaze drifted to his, he had a grin as big as Texas on his face.

This was, she decided, all her grandmother's fault! If she hadn't set that darn cherry pie on the side porch to cool, he would have never come bearing gifts at suppertime, and her grandmother wouldn't have asked him to stay, and he would have never seen her refusal to go out with him as some kind of challenge. This had to stop!

But as much as she wanted to tell Turk in front of God and everyone that he was wasting his time, she knew better. That would only make him more determined. Her gut instinct told her the only way she was going to discourage him was to act completely disinterested.

But how was she supposed to do that when her heart was pounding like crazy and she felt like a sixteen-year-old who'd just been asked out by the captain of the football team? She was losing her mind, she decided. Or suffering from a midlife crisis. She was too old for these kinds of feelings! And she wasn't looking for a man! Why was she having such a difficult time remembering that?

Frustrated, thoroughly disgusted with herself, she tried to ignore the dining area completely and concentrate on the customers lined up for their morning fix of doughnuts and coffee, but that was impossible. Every time she turned toward the cash register, he was right in her line of sight. And she didn't have to see the spark of mischief in his eyes to know that he knew exactly what he was doing to her. Heat climbing her cheeks, she turned quickly away, but not before she saw his grin deepen. Oh, he was enjoying this!

She should have been relieved when he finally left. But when he pushed to his feet and stretched like a lazy cat, her mouth went dry. And when he winked at her and walked out, she knew he'd be back again tomorrow. And her heart thundered just at the thought.

"He's something else, isn't he?" Karen Hudson sighed. "Where was he when I was single? Hell, where was he when I was married the first three times?"

"C'mon, Karen," Rachel chided, shocked. "You and Justin are nuts about each other."

"Of course we are," she retorted. "But I'm not blind, sweetie. And I'll still be appreciating a man like that when I'm a hundred and two. Why in heaven's name aren't you going out with him? And don't tell me you're not interested. Any woman with any blood in her veins would fall all over herself to go out with a man like that. So why aren't you?"

What was she supposed to say to that? "He's not my type," she finally replied, and tried to believe it.

The bell attached to the door rang then, reminding her that she had other customers, and she turned to greet the distraction with a sigh of relief. Then she saw who it was—Mildred Johnson, followed closely by a man who was, no doubt, her nephew, Benny. Mildred had been telling her for weeks that Benny was moving to town, hinting all the while that she hoped that he would find a nice woman and finally settle down. Rachel didn't doubt for a second that Mildred expected her to be that *nice woman*.

Her gaze shifted to the nephew, and she could see why Mildred felt the need to find Benny a date. He wasn't exactly an attractive man. A sloppy dresser who was at least thirty pounds overweight, he was pale as a ghost, had small eyes that were lost behind the thick lenses of his glasses, and he looked as if he hadn't combed his hair in a week. Even if she'd been looking for a man, she wouldn't have gone out with Benny if he'd literally been the last man on earth. And if the continuation of the species had been contingent upon procreating with him, then mankind would have simply ceased to exist—it was that simple.

Mildred, however, wasn't a woman who was easily discouraged. An acquaintance of Rachel's grandmother, she had a reputation for never bending once she'd made up her mind about something. And she'd obviously decided that Rachel was the perfect woman for her nephew.

Oh, she hadn't come right out and said the words, but Rachel wasn't an idiot. She'd been ignoring Mildred's hints about Benny for weeks, and now here he was, God help her.

Wishing she'd called in sick—like she would!—she forced a weak smile as the two of them approached the front counter. "Good morning, Mildred. You're out early this morning."

"I just picked up my nephew at the bus station," she said happily. "He was starving for a decent cup of coffee and a Danish, and I knew you would fix him right up. Rachel, this is Benny." As she turned to her nephew, the usually unyielding lines of her face cracked into an amazingly tender smile. "This is the woman I've been telling you about, sweetheart. I think you two are really going to hit it off."

His beady little eyes swept over Rachel, examining every inch of her. "Well, you're a surprise. I didn't think Aunt Mildred had such good taste."

"Benny really needs someone to show him around town, Rachel," Mildred said eagerly. "I thought maybe you would know someone…"

Rachel wasn't fooled. She expected her to show Benny around and that wasn't happening. "Actually, I don't know anyone," she said lightly, "but if Benny wants to meet people, he should join the Hunter's Ridge Garden Club. From what I understand, there are a lot of single women in the club. I'm sure one of them would be happy to show Benny the sights and introduce him around town."

Mildred frowned, irritation flashing in her eyes. "Oh, but, I was hoping—"

"I don't need to join a garden club to find a woman!"

Aunt and nephew spoke at the same time, making no effort to disguise their annoyance. Rachel could, she supposed, understand why they were more than a little miffed with her, but the sooner they understood that she wasn't the answer to their prayers, the better. "I'm sorry I can't be of more help," she said with wide-eyed innocence, "but I can't think of anyone else. Now, if you'll excuse me, I'm needed in the back. Benny, it was a pleasure meeting you. If you're interested in joining the garden club, someone at the chamber of commerce can tell you when the next meeting is."

Not waiting for a response, she retreated to the kitchen and sent one of her helpers to the front to wait on Mildred and Benny. She didn't come out again until long after they'd left. She was, she knew, acting like a coward, but Mildred was a woman who didn't take no for an answer. She could butt heads with her if she had to, but she preferred to just avoid her. If she steered clear of her long enough, surely Benny would get the message, even if his aunt didn't.

Pleased with the idea, she released a silent sigh

of relief. Then she remembered that glint of smug assurance in Benny's beady little eyes. If he was as determined as his aunt, discouraging him wasn't going to be nearly as easy as she'd hoped.

Rachel always closed the bakery at three-thirty, but after she cleaned up and got things ready for the next morning, it was usually close to five before she got out of there. Today was no different. She'd been on her feet since she rolled out of bed at four in the morning, and she was tired. Later, she and her grandmother and some friends were going out, but for now, she just needed some time to herself to unwind. She couldn't think of a better place to do that than the river. It was only three blocks away and wound through the edge of downtown. Grabbing a bag of breadcrumbs, she started walking.

The ducks saw her first, but then again, they always did. They seemed to have a built-in radar for people who fed them regularly, and the second they saw her cross River Road and enter the narrow strip of land between the river and the road that the city had wisely made into a park, ducks and swans and geese came running.

She'd named them all, of course—she fed them every day—and they all had distinct personalities. "Okay, guys, don't get impatient. There's plenty for everyone. Watch it, Waddles, there's no need to get pushy. Mr. Higgins is going to let you eat. Good boy.

No—that's not yours, Izzy. You've already had more than everyone else. You don't want to be a pig."

Izzy, apparently, disagreed. She pushed herself through the others, gobbling up crumbs so fast, Rachel couldn't help but laugh. "Watch it, girl. Someone's going to snatch you up for Thanksgiving Dinner if you don't slow down. Duck's not real popular in this neck of the woods, but the RV park is full of snowbirds. All it takes is for one of them to get a good look at you and that fat belly of yours, and you're a goner."

Far from concerned, Izzy kept eating as if her life depended on it, pushing her feathered friends out of the way and grabbing every crumb she could for herself.

Amused, Rachel laughed and threw more crumbs.

Out for a run with Daisy, Turk spied Rachel the second he turned onto River Road. Daisy, far more interested in the ducks, gave a sharp bark of excitement and headed right toward them.

"No, Daise," Turk growled. "Behave yourself and leave the ducks alone. They don't want to play."

He might as well have saved his breath. Picking up speed, ignoring his tugs on the leash, Daisy sprinted for Rachel and the ducks.

"No! Daisy, heel!"

A big smile plastered on her doggy face, she never even checked her pace. Swearing, Turk tried to tackle her, but everything was a game to her, and she'd picked up a full head of steam. Dragging him after her, she was twenty yards away and closing fast when Rachel looked up and saw them both bearing down on her.

"Turk! What—"

A split second later, Daisy ran through the gathering of ducks. Turk only had time to note that she made no effort to hurt them when she suddenly saw the bag of breadsticks in Rachel's hand. With an excited bark, she launched herself at her.

"Wait! No!"

Alarmed, her hands extended out to block Daisy from jumping her, Rachel took a step back…and tripped over a rock. A split second later, she went down.

Turk swore. "Dammit, Daisy, now look what you've done! Rachel? Are you okay? Did you hit your head? C'mon, honey, open your eyes and speak to me! Are you hurt?"

Dazed, Rachel opened her eyes and found herself lying flat on her back, looking up at the dog…and Turk. Taking a quick inventory and discovering she wasn't hurt, she wanted to sink right through the hard ground beneath her back. "I can't believe you sicced your dog on me."

"I didn't! I swear!"

"So you can't control your own dog? Is that what you're saying?"

"No, of course not!"

"Then you *did* sic your dog on me."

"You hit your head, didn't you?"

Confused, she frowned. "What's my head got to do with your dog? Why are you changing the subject? Is this a trick question?"

Grinning, he gently helped her sit up. When he slid his fingers through her hair to feel her scalp, she jerked back, a blush heating her cheeks and her dark brows knit together in a scowl. "What are you doing?"

"Checking to make sure you didn't crack your head when Daisy knocked you down," he said, gently inspecting her scalp. "Does this hurt?"

Hurt? she thought, fighting the need to lean into his hand. He couldn't be serious! With just the touch of his fingertips on her scalp, he was turning her boneless. And it wasn't her head that was the problem, anyway. It was her heart. It was slamming against her ribs, and suddenly, she was breathless.

And she knew exactly who to blame. Turk! She could handle the wicked smile and the dancing eyes, but it wasn't fair that he had such a tender touch. She tried to remind herself he was a doctor—he had to be gentle—but it didn't matter. He made her heart trip, and that horrified her. What was wrong with her? This wasn't what she wanted!

"I'm fine," she said hurriedly, only to wince at the huskiness of her voice. Damn the man, did he know what he was doing to her? Suddenly furious with herself and him, she scrambled to her feet and took two quick steps back. "I just wasn't expecting to get attacked by a dog in the park! Don't you know there are leash laws? I've half a mind to report you!"

His lips twitching, Turk held up Daisy's leash. "She was on a leash."

"This isn't funny! I could have been seriously hurt. And what about the ducks? Oh, my God! The ducks! Are they okay?"

She whirled, horrified that Daisy had gone after the ducks while she was making a fool of herself over her owner, but she needn't have worried. The ducks had all scattered when Daisy ran her down and they were now swimming happily in the middle of the river. And Daisy, thankfully, had lost interest in them. She'd found the bag of breadcrumbs she'd knocked out of Rachel's hand and was busily gulping down every smidgen of bread she could find.

Although relieved that the ducks were safe, Rachel became more irritated as she watched Daisy gobble their crumbs. "You're just darn lucky the ducks aren't hurt. They're the town mascots. People are very protective of them. If Daisy had hurt one of them, you'd have been in a world of trouble."

"I'll be more careful next time," he promised, looking suitably contrite. "She was just excited when she saw you. I know how she feels."

Her eyes narrowed dangerously. "Don't go there, Garrison. We're not talking about me."

"No, ma'am. You're absolutely right, ma'am.

But I sure would like to. When do you think we could get together and talk about you over dinner? Just name the time and date and I'll be at your front door with bells on. How about tonight? Or are you the type of woman who likes a couple of days' notice? I'm the spontaneous type, in case you hadn't noticed, but that's one of the little things about you that I don't know. Which is why we need to get together so you can tell me about yourself."

He was getting to her—he could see her fighting a smile—but he had to give her credit for not being a pushover. Her gaze never shying from his, she lifted a delicately arched brow and gave him a cool, superior smile that absolutely delighted him. "Nice try, Garrison. I'm not buying it."

Making no effort to hold back a grin, he quipped, "You have no idea how much I was hoping you'd say that. Did I mention that I love a challenge? Not to mention…a woman with sass. You know, I think we're going to get along just fine."

Ignoring that, she retorted, "Aren't you supposed to be working? I thought your clinic opened today."

"It did—and it's doing great, thank you for asking. But we closed at five, and Daisy needed a run. Are you sure you're all right? No headache? I don't think you should be alone. Daisy and I can keep you company. I'll even cook dinner for you. Of course, we'll have to do it at your house—I'm still tearing out Sheetrock and mine's a mess. Or we could go out—"

That was as far as he got. "There you go again. Don't you ever take no for an answer?"

He grinned. "No."

"I guess we'll have to see about that, won't we?" she said sweetly. "Now, if you'll excuse me, I have to go. I have to get ready for a date."

A slight smile of satisfaction curling her mouth, she turned and grabbed the now-empty bag of breadcrumbs. Not sparing him a single glance, she crossed the street and headed for home.

Watching her until she disappeared from sight, Turk laughed out loud. Well, she'd certainly put him in his place—and thoroughly entertained him at one and the same time. Did she have a clue how much he enjoyed her? Probably not, he thought, chuckling. And she sure as hell wasn't going to let him get close enough to show her. That was okay. He was a man who liked to take his time—he'd get his chance. After all, it wasn't as if she could avoid him forever. He knew where she lived!

Beside him, Daisy whined as she, too, watched Rachel disappear around the corner. "It's okay, girl," he assured her, patting her on the head. "She's not nearly as indifferent as she appears. C'mon, let's go home. I want to see this *date* of hers."

He hadn't spied on a female since he was in junior high, and he should have been shocked that he'd sunk so low. But he wasn't seriously pursing

Rachel, Turk told himself as he began working on the Sheetrock in his living room. She'd thrown down a challenge, he'd picked it up, and he had a sneaking feeling she was enjoying the game as much as he was.

Not that she would admit it, he thought with a grin. From what he could tell, Rachel Martin was a woman who played her cards close to her vest. What would it take to make the lady drop her guard? Finding out was going to be interesting.

Images played in his head, teasing him, distracting him, making it impossible for him to concentrate on his plan to have most of the Sheetrock in the living room demolished by midnight. Instead, he found himself daydreaming about the lady next door…and waiting for her date to arrive.

When he heard a car pull into her driveway an hour later, he moved lightning quick to the front window to get a look at the guy. He wasn't becoming obsessed with Rachel, he assured himself. He was just curious as to what kind of man she found attractive. Obviously, she was sharp as a tack, so she'd go for someone with brains, he decided. Someone who had the sense not to try to boss her around and could make her laugh. As for looks, she was a people person and would probably be more interested in a man's character than his looks.

Outside, the sun had sunk and twilight was

quickly darkening into early evening. Still, it was light enough for Turk to get a good look at the man walking up Rachel's front walk. Stunned, Turk could only stare.

Short and sprightly, his head as bare of hair as a billiard ball, the man had to be eighty, if he was a day.

Confused, Turk frowned. This had to be a joke. Somehow, Rachel had figured out that he was watching and had arranged for some old man to show up on her doorstep as if he was courting her. She couldn't seriously be dating someone old enough to be her grandfather.

But the thought had hardly registered when Rachel opened her front door to her date. Her eyes and smile warm with affection, she laughed when he held out a small paper bag to her and she peaked inside. Delighted, she gave the old man a hug, grinned when he kissed her on the cheek, then linked her arm with his as they made their way to the older-model Oldsmobile parked at the curb. With a gentlemanly, old-fashioned flourish, he opened her car door for her and made sure she was comfortably settled before he walked around the car and climbed in beside her. The Oldsmobile roared to life, and seconds later, they sedately drove down the street and disappeared from view.

Staring after them in disbelief, Turk swore. He would have bet good money that Rachel wasn't the type of woman who fed on vulnerable old men with fat bank accounts and short life spans. Obviously, he was wrong.

Savoring one of the caramels Harvey had brought her, Rachel closed her eyes and smiled as the candy melted in her mouth. "Nobody makes better caramels than you do, Harvey. You know if you sold your recipe to one of the companies that are always hounding you for it, you could sell your candy story and never have to work another day in your life."

"I don't have to work now," he chuckled. "And I can't sell my grandmother's recipe. She and my mama would roll over in their graves. That would be like you selling the recipe to Evelyn's piecrust recipe. Even before she opened the bakery when your daddy was a kid, she had people knocking at her front door all hours of the night and day, wanting to buy one of her pies. She'd have your hide if you gave out that recipe. As far as I know, you're the only one she ever gave it to."

Rachel smiled, remembering the day her grandmother had gotten her piecrust recipe out of the safe and given it to her. "She said she never trusted anyone else to make it right. After she made sure I'd memorized it, she tore up the recipe and burned it in the fireplace. Then she made me promise that I would take just as much care handing it down to my daughter or granddaughter. Not that I'm ever going to have one—"

"Stop that!" he scolded, grinning. "You'll find someone. I'm telling you, sweetheart—you were taught to cook by one of the best. All you have to do is cook for a man and he'll be yours, just like that."

"If that's the case, then why haven't you ever married?" she countered. "You're a darn good cook yourself, and you can make your own candy. You don't need me to tell you that most women can't even make candy. So why haven't you gone out and found one with a sweet tooth?"

His smile faded. "I found the right one years ago," he confided. "She doesn't know I'm alive, except as a friend."

"Who…?" His meaning finally hit her, and she gasped, "You mean *Gran?* You're in love with Gran?"

A wry, crooked smile curved the corners of his mouth. "It's a lost cause, I know, but I have been for years."

"Oh, Harvey! Have you told her?"

"No, and I'm not going to. I knew a long time ago that she would never love anyone but Clarence."

"But you should tell her!"

"Oh, no!" he said quickly. "And you've got to promise that you won't, either! Then she'd be uncomfortable around me and I'd lose her friendship. I won't risk that."

"But—"

"No buts, Rachel. Stop and think about it. You know what a mass of contradictions she is. She went out and opened her own business at a time when women didn't work outside the home, but she's a stickler about her reputation. She won't even ride in my car without a chaperone, honey. What do you think she'd do if she knew that all these years, when I came over to the house to fix a leaky faucet for her or mow the grass or clean out the gutters, that I was in love with her?

"She'd freak," Rachel agreed, "which is ridiculous. It's the twenty-first century, for heaven's sake! No one's going to talk about her if she rides around town with you in your car."

He grinned. "I know that and you know that, but here I am, picking you up first so that no one will talk about her."

"And it doesn't seem to enter her head that if people are going to talk about her, it won't be for riding around town with you. It'll be because she's a secret card shark who plays poker ever Saturday night!"

Chapter 5

"Well, you two certainly seem to be in a fine mood," Evelyn said as they arrived at her house to pick her up. "What's going on?"

"Nothing," Harvey said easily. "Rachel was just keeping me entertained. I see you've got your red shoes on. Feeling lucky, are you?"

"I've had them on all day," she retorted, grinning. "So be forewarned. I'm going to beat the socks off of both of you."

"You think so, do you? Well, I guess we'll just have to see about that, won't we? Did I mention that I had a dream last night—"

"Here we go," she teased. "Another one of your

psychic dreams. So what'd you dream this time? That you're going to win the lottery? You have to play first, sweetie."

"That's okay, enjoy your fun," he retorted. "Winning the lottery isn't always about buying a ticket."

When her grandmother frowned, trying to figure that one out, Harvey just winked at Rachel and said, "Time's a-wasting and Lawrence is probably wondering where we are. You girls ready?"

"I just have to get the peach cobbler," Evelyn said, heading for the kitchen. "Did you remember to pick up the fried chicken?"

"It's in the car," he assured her.

"Along with the potato salad I made," Rachel added. "I'll warn you ahead of time—it's tart. Just about the best I ever made."

"Stop," her grandmother laughed. "You're making me hungry! Let's get out of here before we decide to eat right here!"

"That sounds good to me," Harvey quipped. "Then we don't have to share with Lawrence."

"Harvey!"

Laughing at both women's horrified exclamation, he hurried them outside to his car, then drove across town to Lawrence's house. The other man was watching for them, and the second they pulled into the driveway, he stepped outside to help carry the food in.

"You're late," he greeted them. "You ate without me, didn't you."

"Harvey wanted to," Rachel retorted, her blue eyes dancing with mischief. "Personally, I don't know how you can be friends with the man. He was going to cut you out, Lawrence, just like that."

Not the least bit disturbed, he chuckled. "That's okay, I ate his share of the deviled eggs while I was waiting for you guys."

"You did not!"

"I was hungry—"

"He's bluffing," Evelyn said, studying him shrewdly. "Look at his left eye. It always twitches when he's bluffing. You really have to work on that, Lawrence."

Not the least bit put out that she'd seen through the lie, he grinned. "Yeah, but I had you going for a while, didn't I?"

For an answer, Harvey gave him a friendly shove. "Next time, I really am eating your chicken."

The poker game began promptly at seven-thirty, just as it had every Saturday night for the past four months. Rachel had come up with the idea of starting the game—not only was the whole country going crazy over the game, but there was some evidence that it helped keep the mind sharp and possibly warded off Alzheimer's in later years. When Rachel told her grandmother and her friends the statistics, that was all the encouragement they needed to start a weekly game. And she had to give them credit—they weren't just going through the motions. They played to win, and in spite of Lawrence's poor attempt at bluffing, they had all become quite good at winning with outrageously poor hands.

"Why don't we plan a trip to Vegas next month?" Evelyn suggested as Lawrence dealt the first hand and Harvey rationed the same number of peanuts to everyone. "I think it's time we found out if we're any good or not."

"I don't know about that, Gran," Rachel said with a frown. "That's a little ambitious, don't you think? Maybe it would be better if we get our feet wet with a local competition, instead."

"Yeah, I heard there was a big competition in Austin in a couple of weeks. Why don't we try that?"

"I'll check the Internet and see how much the entrance fee is," Harvey said. "I'll drive, if you like."

"Are you kidding?" Lawrence scoffed. "I've ridden with you on the interstate, remember? We'll let Rachel drive. She's got better eyes than the three of us put together."

"In that case, you won't mind if I suggest that you stop dealing from the bottom of the deck," Rachel said dryly. "I don't know about the rest of you, but I prefer my cards from the top."

"Whatever you say, sweetheart," he told her with

a wink as he immediately dealt the rest of the cards from the top of the deck. "Just checking to see if anyone's paying attention."

"We appreciate that," Evelyn said dryly. Checking her cards, she grinned at Lawrence. "Thanks for the hand. I'll see your five and raise you twenty."

Harvey eyed her speculatively. "I think you're bluffing. I'll see your twenty and raise you ten."

Her face carefully blank of expression, Rachel studied her grandmother and her card-shark buddies over the top of her cards, fighting a grin all the while. Personally, she thought they were both bluffing, and Lawrence had to know that...because he'd dealt her a straight flush.

"Well, Rachel?" Lawrence asked, just a hint of a smile tugging at his lips. "Fish or cut bait, sweetheart. What's it going to be?"

"I'm debating," she replied, knowing very well he knew she wasn't. "It's going to be a long evening. I don't want to risk everything on the first hand."

"Study long, you study wrong," Harvey quipped. "Not that it matters, you're not going to win this hand, anyway."

"You're probably right about that, but I'll try...just for fun." She tossed in her peanuts, then raised eyebrows when she refused more cards. "I'll go with the ones I have, thanks."

The others looked at one another, exchanged

knowing glances, then immediately folded. "C'mon, guys! This isn't fair!"

"You never hold all your cards unless you've got a pat hand, sweetheart," her grandmother chuckled. "What've you got?"

"Just a straight flush," she retorted, grinning. "After listening to the three of you—*two* of you," she corrected when Lawrence loudly cleared his throat, "I felt sure one of you was bound to have a royal flush."

For an answer, her grandmother and Harvey both threw down their cards. Between the two of them, they didn't have a single pair, let alone anything close to a straight or a flush.

Laughing, Evelyn reached for the cards. "My deal!"

It was after midnight when Harvey walked Rachel to her door and made sure she was safely inside before heading home himself. The night had been fun, but then again, she'd known that it would be. Harvey and Lawrence always treated her like a favorite granddaughter, and they never failed to make her laugh. And she'd won! She had a purse full of peanuts, and even though her bluffing skills still needed work, she couldn't complain.

Until she looked out of her bedroom window and her eyes fell on Turk's house. Through his bare windows, she could see him working on the Sheetrock in his living room. Didn't the man ever sleep? she wondered, irritated for reasons she couldn't begin to explain. It was almost one o'clock in the morning! If he started hammering, she was going to give him a piece of her mind!

But ten minutes later when she turned out her bedroom light and crawled into bed, only silence greeted her ears. Relieved, she pulled the covers up and sighed as her eyes drifted shut. Within two ticks of the clock, she was sound asleep.

Hours later, she was still dead to the world when the rumbling growl of a truck pulled at her consciousness. Squinting at the clock on her bedside table, she groaned when she saw that it was barely seven in the morning. What idiot was out and about so early in the morning? Didn't they know this was her one morning to sleep late? Rolling over, she buried her head under her pillow and sighed in contentment as she drifted back to sleep.

"Come on back! You've got plenty of room. Just watch the trees. Yeah, you're doing great! Another few feet—"

Rachel's eyes popped open at the sound of Turk, yelling at someone over the sound of a truck making an incredible racket, apparently right outside her bedroom window! "What the—"

"Watch it! You're only a couple of feet from the yard light! You need to move to the left. Yeah, that's it—"

"No, that's not it!" Rachel retorted, throwing back her covers. Irritating man! It was seven o'clock in the morning, dammit! *Sunday* morning! Had he lost his mind?

"Inconsiderate oaf!" she muttered as she jerked on her robe and jammed her bare feet into her house shoes. "Was he raised in a barn? Obviously, he thinks he's the only one on the damn planet. Just wait. When I get through with him, he's going to wish he was!"

Fuming, she stormed outside, uncaring that her hair was flying and she hadn't even taken the time to wash her face. The second she spied him standing in his driveway as if it was the middle of the afternoon, directing the truck driver, who was changing the overflowing Dumpster in his driveway for an empty one, she saw red. *"Do you know what time it is?"*

Over the roar of the diesel truck and the clang of the empty Dumpster, Turk couldn't hear a thing. But he caught a glimpse of movement out of the corner of his eye and glanced up in time to see Rachel bearing down on him with a look in her blue eyes that would have sent the bravest man running for the hills. Turk only grinned and yelled a cheery "Good morning!"

"You woke me up! Dammit, this is the only day of the week I can sleep late!"

Turk heard every word, but he only cupped his hand to his ear and said, "What? I can't hear you!"

"It's Sunday!" she yelled back in growing frustration. "You woke me up!"

Cupping his hand to his ear, he shrugged, then pointed to the Dumpster, which the driver had started to lower to the ground, and shrugged his shoulders in an age-old gesture that told her without words that he couldn't hear a thing she was saying. And this time, he wasn't pretending. The noise was tremendous. She was left with no choice but to watch.

She was so frustrated, Turk could almost feel the air humming, and it was all he could do not to laugh.

When the Dumpster hit the ground with a clattering loud enough to wake the dead, Rachel jumped, swearing, and glared at Turk. "Hey, it's not my fault the truck is so loud," he told her, but he might as well have saved his breath. The truck driver chose that moment to rev his motor, honk his horn and drive off, grinding his gears as he rumbled down the street.

Wincing, Turk grinned. "Sorry about that. So what was it you were saying?"

"What was I *saying?*" she sputtered. "What do you think I was saying? Do you know what time it is? Obviously not, or you wouldn't be *waking everyone in the neighborhood!*"

The volume of her voice went up with every word until she was practically shouting at him. She was in a fine temper, and Turk couldn't say he blamed her. It *was* early, and when he'd ordered a clean Dumpster, he hadn't stopped to think just how noisy the delivery would be...or that his neighbors might not appreciate the early delivery time.

"Look, I'm sorry. I never dreamed it would be so loud—"

"It's Sunday, for heaven's sake!" she fumed. "The only day of the week some people get to sleep! But do you care? Do you even warn people?"

"I—"

"No! You just have the thing hauled in here and make enough noise to wake the dead!"

"And I've apologized for that. But I needed to change out the Dumpster, and today was the only day I had open to have it delivered. I had to pay extra for a Sunday delivery."

"*Extra?*" she sputtered. "You paid *extra* to disturb everyone within a five-block radius?"

Not the least disturbed that she was furious with him, Turk couldn't take his eyes off her. Grinning, he wondered if she knew how her eyes flashed with temper when she was in a snit? Or that her cheeks were flushed, her hair wild? He definitely liked the way she looked when she got right out of bed. Did she realize she was standing before him in nothing but a gown and robe? She didn't have a lick of makeup on...and couldn't have managed to look more beautiful if she'd tried.

"Are you listening to me? Don't you have anything to say for yourself?"

"As a matter of fact I do," he retorted gruffly. And with no more warning than that, he reached for her and hauled her into his arms.

He hadn't planned to kiss her, hadn't planned to touch her at all. But there was just something about her that he found incredibly appealing…especially when she stood toe to toe with him and gave him a piece of her mind. He liked a woman who stood up for herself. He liked the challenge in her eyes, the jut of her stubborn chin, the flush in her cheeks. But most of all, he liked the taste of her—

Suddenly realizing that he was kissing the stuffing out of her—and she was kissing him back!—he regained his senses with a jolt. What the devil was he doing? He'd just meant to tease her…not lose himself in her! Had he forgotten what had happened with Laureen so quickly? That's how his problems with her had started, with just a little kiss, and he'd been regretting it ever since. He wasn't going there again, not with a woman he barely knew. And he certainly wasn't getting involved with anyone right now, not when he was still trying to establish his practice and remodel his house and start his life over. He just didn't have time.

That didn't mean, however, that he wouldn't spend a heck of a lot of time thinking about this particular kiss…and this particular woman.

Regret tugging at him, he stepped back only to almost reach for her again when she looked up at him dazedly. Who would have thought Miss in Control Martin could be thrown into confusion with just a kiss?

Amused, his own pounding heart his secret to keep, he made no attempt to hold back a grin. "Don't look at me like that, sweetheart, or I'll think you want me to kiss you again."

Her eyes snapped at that, delighting him. "Okay, that's more like it," he said approvingly. "There's the woman I like to tease and torment. I thought I'd lost you for a minute."

Still reeling from his kiss, she gave serious consideration to shooting the man. Unfortunately, that had been illegal for quite some time, so all she could do was glare at him and pray that he couldn't hear the still-crazy pounding of her heart. "Don't flatter yourself," she said coolly. "In case you don't recognize it when you see it, that was nothing but pure indifference."

Far from insulted, he only grinned. "Really? Sounds like a throw down to me."

When he took a step toward her, she would have given anything to just stand there and let him kiss her without showing an ounce of emotion. But her heart was still jumping, her knees trembling, and if he touched her again, kissed her again, she knew the last thing she would be was indifferent.

Taking a quick step back, she said, "Oh, no you don't. You keep your hands and your lips to yourself, Turk Garrison! Stay away from me! Do you hear me? You stay on your side of your property line and I'll stay on mine, and we'll both get along fine!"

His aforementioned lips twitched. "In case you hadn't noticed, Miss Martin, you're on my side of the property line."

Heat singed her cheeks. She was, dammit! Her chin held high, she stepped onto her own property and confronted him from the relatively safe distance of twenty feet away. "There! I trust I have made myself clear?"

"Completely, sweetheart," he chuckled. "I make you nervous."

He couldn't begin to know how much. Infuriated that he could read her so easily, she sniffed, "There you go again, flattering yourself. You really should do something about that ego of yours. Now, if you'll excuse me, I'd like to get some sleep before the morning is completely gone."

Without another word, she turned and stormed off. With every step, she could feel his eyes on her, the touch of his infuriating grin, and that only irritated her more. Impossible man! she fumed. He was a tease and a flirt and he knew just what to say and do to make her heart pound. That didn't mean she was interested in him. It was just chemistry. She wasn't interested in anyone. She just wanted a baby. So why was she having such a difficult time remembering that whenever she got within twenty feet of Turk Garrison? There had to be some way to get the man out of her head.

Avoid him, the irritating voice in her head

retorted. *It shouldn't be that difficult. You know where the man works, where he spends his days, where he lives, for heaven's sake! When you see him, turn and go the other direction.*

That sounded so easy. And it would have been…with anyone else but Turk. He turned up at the bakery every morning, and in spite of her resolve not to wait on him, she found herself face-to-face with him across the counter, serving him coffee and doughnuts. He came by the river when she fed the ducks, carried broken pieces of Sheetrock out to the Dumpster in his driveway when she dragged her trashcans to the curb on garbage day, and grinned at her whenever he passed her on the street.

That, however, wasn't the worst of it. She couldn't get him out of her head. She found herself looking for him everywhere she went, listening for him when he arrived home after a long day at the clinic, catching glimpses of him in line at the grocery store and post office and bank. She had to be losing her mind.

In growing desperation, she went out with an old friend who was newly divorced and just looking for a way to forget her ex-husband. Hoping to meet someone, *anyone*, who might take her mind off Turk and get her back on track in her hunt for a sperm donor, Rachel wore black slacks and a red spaghetti-strap camisole that was sparkly and sexy and eye-popping. She might as well have worn a duster. In spite of the fact that the uptown bar they went to had a live band and seemed to be overflowing with good-looking, successful men, she just wasn't in the mood.

Discouraged, she called it quits after two hours of torture and headed home. What was wrong with her? she wondered as she pulled into her driveway and cut the engine. All she wanted to do was go inside and cry. Nothing was working out as she'd planned and she didn't understand why.

Lost in her own misery, she stepped out of her car and didn't see Turk sitting on his front porch in the darkness until a car unexpectedly turned the corner and its headlights swept across both Turk's yard and hers. In the sudden flash of bright lights, she suddenly spied him on his porch, just sitting in a wooden rocker, gently rocking back and forth. His eye met hers and clung, even after the car disappeared down the street, leaving them, once again, surrounded by darkness.

She could barely see him sitting in the shadows, but she knew his eyes were locked with hers. She had nothing to say to him—she should have just nodded and gone into the house. But her heart was knocking against her ribs, and the kiss that she'd been trying to forget for days was suddenly right there between them, setting the night air pulsing with an emotion she refused to put a name to.

Suddenly breathless, her head and heart reeling, she couldn't have moved if her life had depended on it.

Later, she didn't know how long she would have stood there, caught in the heat of the memory, if Daisy hadn't suddenly spotted her from Turk's backyard and started to bark. Snapping back to her surroundings, she hurried inside without sparing Turk another glance.

Her house was quiet, dark, empty. Standing in the shadowy darkness of her living room, she'd never felt so lonely in her life. All she wanted to do was go to bed and cry herself to sleep. Heading for her bedroom, she flipped on the light and started to change into her nightgown, only to remember that tomorrow was trash pickup and she hadn't put the cans out at the road. She wouldn't have time to do it in the morning—getting to the bakery by four-thirty every morning left her no time to do anything but throw on some clothes and put on her makeup.

"Damn!" Swearing softly, she quickly changed out of her dating finery into jeans and a T-shirt. Then she flipped on lights as she moved from one room to another, making her way through the house as she collected the trash.

Sitting in the darkness on his front porch, Turk watched the lights go on and off, room by room, in Rachel's house. What the heck was she doing? he wondered. He'd watched her leave earlier and hadn't been able to stop thinking about her since. She'd been dressed for trouble when she'd left, and he'd taken one look at her and forgotten to breathe. Did the woman know how hot she was? Or what trouble she could get into dressed in that sexy top?

He'd been worrying about her ever since she left, looking out the front windows to see if she was back again, watching the clock. Irritated with himself, he'd finally gone out on the front porch to wait for her, just like an overanxious father waiting on a teenage daughter out on the town for the first time. And that irritated the hell out of him. What was wrong with him? He hardly knew her, damn it!

And his feelings for her were anything but paternal.

His jaw tightened just at the thought of her bringing some jerk home with her, but she'd come home alone. And that irritated him even more. What was wrong with the men of Hunter's Ridge? Didn't they have eyes in their head? She was gorgeous... and, apparently, available. Why weren't they lined up at the bakery every morning, asking her out like he was?

Maybe because she shot them down just like she did you!

A reluctant grin tugged at his mouth at the thought. Okay, so she was no pushover. Any man with any brains in his head would find that incredibly attractive, not to mention damn challenging. He certainly did.

Which was why he was sitting on his front porch like a Peeping Tom, watching the lights go on, then off, in her house.

Shaking his head—when had he sunk to this level?—he pushed to his feet. It was time to call it a night. She was safe and snug in her own home, and he didn't have to worry about her anymore.

But before he could move, the floodlights next door were flipped on and Rachel stepped outside, carrying a bag of trash. She carried it to the curb, then immediately headed for the old-fashioned, detached garage behind the house, where her trash cans were stored.

Watching her, Turk knew he should have let her carry the cans to the curb herself. She obviously didn't want to speak to him, and while he wouldn't have normally let that stop him, there was something about her solemn expression, the slight slump of her shoulders, that told him her evening hadn't gone as planned. She looked down, sad, lonely. Frowning, he took one look at her face and found himself heading straight for her.

"Need some help?"

Obviously caught up in her thoughts, she didn't see him striding toward her until he spoke. Startled, she jumped. "What? No! I'm fine—I can get it."

"Are you sure? You can take one side, and I'll get the other.

"It's not that heavy," she insisted, but when she

tried to lift the can on her own, she grunted at the effort it took just to pick it up an inch off the ground.

"You are so stubborn," he chuckled, nudging her out of the way. "Here. Let me do that." Stepping around her, he picked up the can himself, only to grunt in surprise. "What the devil have you got in here? Rocks?"

The corner of her mouth turned up into a half smile. "Actually, it's just some old magazines. I couldn't sleep the other night, so I decided to clean out some things. I guess I got carried away."

"You got that right," he chuckled. Huffing and puffing, he carried the trash can to the curb. "There! What about the other one? Did you need that one carried to the curb, too?"

"Oh, no," she assured him quickly. "Just the one, tonight. But thanks, anyway."

"No problem," he said easily. He should have wished her good-night and gone inside then, but his curiosity had always gotten him into trouble, and tonight was no different. "So how was your date?"

She shot him a sharp look. "Who said I had a date? Have you been spying on me?"

A crooked grin propped up one corner of his mouth. "I don't have to spy, Rachel. All I have to do is look out the window. You looked…hot."

He was the one and only man to notice all evening. Why did that set her heart somersaulting in her breast? "I didn't have a date," she admitted huskily. "I just went out with an old girlfriend whose divorce was final today. She wanted to see if she still had what it took to attract a man."

"And did she?"

A slight smile warmed her eyes. "Let's just say she didn't have to buy her own drinks. That's a start."

"And what about you?"

Surprised, she blinked. "What about me?"

"Who bought your drinks?"

"I did." Suddenly realizing that she was discussing her private life with a man who was little more than a stranger to her, she stiffened. "It's late," she said coolly. "I have to go in."

Watching her walk away, Turk wanted to ask her if she paid her own way because no one else offered or if she preferred it that way, but he already knew the answer. Rachel Martin was a woman who leaned on no one.

Chapter 6

In the dead of night, the phone rang sharply, cutting through the quiet stillness that shrouded the house. Startled, Turk jerked awake and squinted at the clock on his nightstand. It was 2:00 a.m. Swearing, he fumbled for the phone on his nightstand. "This better be good."

"Poor baby. Did I wake you?"

Already drifting back to sleep, he stiffened, his blood suddenly ice cold. Laureen. He would have recognized her voice in the depths of hell. How the devil had she gotten his phone number? It was restricted.

"What do you want, Laureen?"

"Just you, sweetheart," she purred. "You're all

I've ever wanted. Why haven't you called me? You promised you would once you were settled."

"I've been busy," he retorted. "It takes a lot of work to set up a new practice."

"Of course it does—which is why you should have taken me with you. I would have helped you hire your staff. And who's doing your decorating, sweetheart? Please tell me you didn't get one of those stuffed shirts who specializes in medical and dental offices. They'll make your waiting room look like a morgue. You want something warm and cozy and homey. Why don't you let me help you?"

"How did you get my phone number, Laureen?"

"I'm a resourceful girl, sweetheart," she laughed. "You know that. That's why you didn't give me your new number. You wanted to see if I could find it on my own."

"I didn't give it to you because I didn't want you to have it," he said bluntly. "We're not dating. We're not a couple. I don't know how many times I have to tell you that."

"You're just afraid," she said easily. "And I don't know why. It's not like I'm going to hurt you or anything. The first time I laid eyes on you, I knew you were the one I'd been waiting for all my life."

"Don't—"

"It's okay, sweetheart. I know you're not ready to talk about your feelings for me yet, and that's okay. Take all the time you need. I can wait. I know

we'll be together in the end. Now...tell me about
the house. What's it look like? Am I going to like
it? How big is the bedroom? Does it have a fireplace? If it doesn't, that's okay. We can put one in.
I want our bedroom to be the most romantic place
in the world. I've been looking at bedding—"

His blood running cold, Turk didn't even try to
stop her. Her voice soft and husky and eerily seduc-
tive, she described a bedroom that sounded like a
silken trap, complete with candles and wine and
mirrors on the ceiling. They would spend hours
together, days, making love, locked away from the
world and needing no one but each other.

Another woman would have teased him with the
fantasy, made it a joke when she realized he wasn't
interested, and dropped it. But this was no joke to
Laureen. Somehow, some way, she intended to make
her fantasy come true—it was just a matter of time.

And that scared the hell out of him. She was a
sick puppy. He'd never personally had any dealings
with a stalker, but he suspected Laureen had all the
markings of one. She already had his phone number.
Did she have his address, also? What exactly was
the woman capable of?

Not willing to go there, he rudely broke into her
fantasy. "There is no us, Laureen. You have to listen
to me. We only went out a couple of times. I'm not
in love with you."

He expected an explosion of anger, but she only

chuckled. "Stop teasing, silly. I know you fell in love with me the minute you laid eyes on me. I saw it in your eyes."

"No, you did not," he said firmly. "I don't love you. I never loved you. I never will love you. I'm not trying to be cruel, but I can't let you continue this fantasy. You need to move on with your life and find someone else. I have."

He hadn't, of course. He was just telling her that. There was no relationship—they'd gone out to dinner twice, end of story. That hardly constituted a relationship. And he had moved on…to Hunter's Ridge, to his own practice, his own home, to—

Rachel.

The thought came from out of the blue, nearly knocking him out of his shoes. What the devil was wrong with him? He didn't have a relationship was Rachel! He hardly knew her. Okay, so he'd spent the last few days pressuring her to go out with him. He liked her—

Images of the kiss he'd given her floated before his mind's eye, teasing him, heating his blood. Okay, he thought with a silent groan, he more than liked the woman. He was attracted to her. He wanted to take her out. He wanted to—

"What do you mean…you've *moved on?*" Laureen asked sharply, jerking him out of his own fantasy. "You can't! You're mine! Who is she? What's her name? Damn it, Turk, tell me!"

Her rage was instantaneous, like a tornado that dropped out of a clear sky. Stunned, Turk almost dropped the phone. Screaming obscenities at him, she called him every name in the book.

Another man might have tried to reason with her, but he wasn't a psychiatrist and she needed the kind of help he couldn't give her. Without a word, he quietly hung up, then turned off all his phones. Tomorrow, he'd call the phone company and change not only his home phone number, but his cell... again. He didn't doubt that she'd find a way to get the new numbers, but hopefully, it would take her a while. In the meantime, he was going to also talk to his lawyer about a restraining order...just in case he needed one in the future.

The third Saturday of October, antique dealers from around the state brought their treasures to town for Market Days and set up booths on the square. It was always Rachel's favorite weekend of the year. Leaving her employees in charge of the bakery, she headed for the square at dawn, her VW Bug loaded for bear with equipment and pastries, and quickly began to set up her booth. Other venders were doing the same, and soon the square was thriving with life as bargain hunters and tourists who flocked to Hunter's Ridge for a day of antiquing hit the streets.

Decorating her booth with a garland of autumn leaves, Rachel had just opened for business when her first customer of the day stopped by. "I knew it! You're handling everything by yourself again this year, aren't you?" Libby Dunkin scolded as she stepped forward to help her with the garland. "I told Henry you needed help, so don't tell me you've got it all under control. I've got eyes, girl. Why didn't you make Mick come with you? Or Jenny? There's no telling what you're paying those lazy bums—make them work for their salary!"

"They do work," she chuckled. "They're holding the fort down at the bakery and making sure I have everything I need. When I get low on doughnuts, Mick makes runs over here so I don't have to leave the booth."

"And who helps you when you get snowed under with customers?" she retorted, nodding toward the people who were already lining up. "You need help, missy. Did you bring another apron?"

For an answer, Rachel handed her one of the spares she'd brought with her. "Only if you let me pay you, though."

"Oh, no you don't! You just donate that money to a charity or something. I don't need it."

Her blue eyes twinkling, Rachel made no effort to hold back a grin. "Well, if that's the way you want it. I was going to give you a pecan pie to take home to Henry, but if you don't want it—"

"What? Did you say pecan pie? Of course I want it! Henry would have my hide, girl, if he knew I turned down a pie from you. Especially pecan! What do you want me to do? Just say the word."

"You keep track of the money and I'll take care of the inventory."

"Sounds good to me," she said, taking a seat behind the table where Rachel had set up the change box. "Let's get started."

The next customer in line bought a dozen doughnuts and an equal number of pigs in a blanket. The rush was on. For the next two hours, neither Rachel nor Libby had time to take a deep breath.

When the rush ended as quickly as it had begun, Libby collapsed in her chair like a wilted flower. "Finally! I was beginning to think we were never going to get a break!"

"Now you know what it's like at the bakery every morning," Rachel said with a laugh. "Why don't you go stretch your legs while you can and take a break? I can handle things for now."

She didn't have to tell her twice. "I won't be gone long," she promised.

"Take your time. I'll be fine."

Taking advantage of the lull, Rachel took a quick inventory of the products she hadn't yet sold, restocked the shelves with her vastly depleted supplies, then called the bakery for a delivery. There would, she knew, be a big rush around one, when people would want dessert after eating lunch. Then Libby would see what a true rush was.

"Rachel! There you are! I was just telling Benny that you always set up a booth for market days. Doesn't she look pretty, Benny?"

"Yeah, she does, Aunt Mildred," he said obediently. "I like her red sweater. It's nice and tight."

"Benny! Stop that! You shouldn't talk like that to Rachel. Apologize immediately."

"Of course," he said smoothly. "I'm sorry, Rachel. I hope I didn't offend you. Let me make it up to you and take you out to dinner. You name the day, the time, the place, and we'll go."

"That's a wonderful idea, sweetheart!" Mildred exclaimed, pleased. "You should take her to the new restaurant on Second Avenue—the Bistro. I've heard it's excellent. I'm sure you'll love it, Rachel."

Not with Benny Johnson, Rachel thought in revulsion. "I can't," she said flatly.

"But why?"

"You have to have lunch," he pointed out. "We can go one day on your lunch break."

What did it take to get through to these people? Rachel wondered. She'd told them time after time she wasn't interested, but they refused to listen, and she was sick of it!

Desperate to make them both realize once and for all that she was never, ever, going to go out with Benny, she said, "I didn't want to tell you this—I didn't want to hurt anyone's feelings—but I can't go out with Benny because I'm dating someone else."

"Who?" Mildred demanded harshly, scowling. "Hunter's Ridge isn't that big, Rachel. If you were dating someone, I would have heard about it."

"He's new in town," she retorted. "You wouldn't know him. The minute I met him, I knew he was the one. I'm sorry, Benny, but—"

"She's taken," Turk said smoothly, coming up behind her to slip an arm around her waist and pull her close. His blue eyes dancing with mischief when she jumped in surprise, he grinned. "Hi, sweetheart. Sorry I'm late. I had an emergency at the clinic this morning. So introduce me to your friends."

He was enjoying himself far too much, but Rachel had never been so glad to see anyone in her life. "Mildred, Benny…this is Turk Garrison. He's the new doctor in town."

Mildred looked like she'd swallowed a pickle at that, but she forced a weak smile. "I read about the new clinic in the paper. I didn't realize you and Rachel were…."

"Dating?" he supplied with a crooked smile when she hesitated. "I asked her out the first time I laid eyes on her. Didn't I, sweetheart?"

Heat climbing in her cheeks, Rachel couldn't deny it. "Yes, he did. He was quite a pest."

"That's what she loves about me," he confided to Benny.

"Turk—"

"It's true, sweetheart," he said at her protest. "She

can't resist a tease," he told Benny with a wink. "Lucky for me, huh? So…Benny, what do you do?"

"He's in insurance," his aunt answered for him. "And quite successful."

"I'm sure," Turk replied. "He seems to have the personality for it. And it is one of the necessary evils of life, you know."

Mildred gasped at that. "I beg your pardon."

"Well, somebody should. I'm paying a fortune in medical malpractice insurance and just making the insurance companies richer. It's a racket, but I guess there's not much Benny can do about that except keep pocketing those premiums. But you're not here to discuss business, are you?

"How about some cookies?" he asked with an innocent look he must have spent years practicing in front of a mirror. "Or a pie? My Rachel-pooh makes the most incredible cherry pie. Evelyn taught her. I suppose you two know Evelyn? She's a sweetheart, isn't she? She put in a good word for me when Rachel wouldn't give me the time of day. You should call her, Benny. I bet she could help you meet a nice woman. She seems to know everyone in town. Of course, Rachel's one of a kind, but there's bound to be some nice single women in Hunter's Ridge. Have you tried going to church?"

Mildred gasped, outraged. "You have some nerve!"

Far from offended, he only grinned. "You know, I've been told that by a number of people,

usually when they don't get what they want out of
me or someone I care about. Is that why you're so
upset, Mrs. Johnson? Because I'm in the way of
Benny asking Rachel out? Too bad. Let him get
his own woman."

Rachel's mine.

He didn't say the words, but Rachel heard them,
nevertheless. With heat climbing in her cheeks, she
shot him a warning look, but before she could say
a word, Mildred huffed, "If this is the kind of man
you're attracted to, Rachel, then it's a good thing
Benny found out now. He's nothing like that, and
the two of you would have never suited. C'mon,
Benny. Let's get out of here. From now on, we'll go
to Fran Steven's bakery when we want any pastries.
Her doughnuts are better, anyway."

His black eyes cold as they swept over Rachel,
Benny said, "I think you're right, Aunt Mildred.
Rachel obviously isn't the woman she led us to
believe she was. Isn't that Tanya Petty looking at the
miniature windmills? Let's go talk to her."

They left without sparing Rachel or Turk another
glance, hurrying across the square as if the hounds
of hell were after them. Watching them greet Tanya
as if she was Benny's long-lost love, Rachel felt as
if she'd just won the lottery. Laughing, she impulsively threw herself into Turk's arms. "Thank you!
Thank you! *Thank you!* My God, do you know what
you've done?"

"Hopefully, gotten rid of that obnoxious woman and her worm of a nephew," he laughed. "That is what you wanted, isn't it?"

"Oh, my God, yes! Mildred has been trying to set me up with Benny for months, long before he even moved to town. I kept telling her I wasn't interested, but it was like talking to the wall!" Thrilled that the pressure was off, she pulled back to grin up at him. "Did I say thank you? You'll never know how much I appreciate this."

"My pleasure," he chuckled. "Anything to help a lady. So, now that we're a couple, when are we going out?"

His blue eyes laughed into hers, warming her all the way to her toes and setting alarm bells clanging in her head. "Turk—"

At her warning tone, he pressed a hand to his heart and sighed. "Be still my heart. I love it when you say my name that way."

"Turk!"

"You did it again. Tell me you're crazy about me. You know you are."

She just barely bit back a grin. "You're terrible, do you know that? I'm trying to be serious—"

"So am I, sweetheart. You're just playing hard to get."

Across the square, Evelyn watched Rachel and Turk laughing and talking, and she couldn't have been more pleased. "Lookie there, boys," she told her poker-playing buddies. "Can you believe it? I do believe our Rachel is flirting with the new doctor in town and she doesn't even know it."

"Well, don't tell her," Lawrence said.

"God, no!" Harvey agreed. "You know how she is. She'll deny it, then avoid the man altogether because—"

"She doesn't want a man!" Evelyn and Lawrence said together, grinning.

"Poor baby," Harvey chuckled. "She just doesn't realize that's exactly what she needs."

Her eyes still trained on her granddaughter, Evelyn laughed. "And she can't avoid this one. He lives right next door!"

"And he's a doctor, hmm?" Harvey said, studying Turk. "I think I'll go check him out."

A frown knitting his brow, Lawrence nodded. "Good idea. We need to make sure he's not anything like that jerk of an ex-husband of hers. She's been hurt enough."

"Just be subtle!" Evelyn called after them. "Don't scare him off. He's a nice guy!"

"Hi, sweetheart. Have you got some brownies for a couple of old men?"

Whirling, Rachel grinned. "Of course I do! And you're not old men. Where have you guys been? I expected you hours ago."

"Harvey doesn't move as fast as he used to," Lawrence said with twinkling eyes. "Of course, he's older than I am, so that's to be expected."

Harvey rolled his eyes. "I'm three weeks older than the old goat, for God's sake! Ask anyone— they'll tell you I look ten years younger!"

"Yeah, right! And I'm the Easter Bunny!" Pointedly looking at her companion, he lifted a gray brow. "So aren't you going to introduce us to your friend?" Not giving her the chance, he extended his hand for a shake. "You're new in town, aren't you?"

"Of course he's new," Harvey retorted. "If he wasn't, we'd know him. I'm Harvey Snyder," he told Turk. "And this is Lawrence Jones. And you're…?"

"Turk Garrison," he said, grinning as he shook hands with the two of them. "I bought the house next door to Rachel."

"Oh! You're the one with the Dumpster out front?"

"With the dog that ate Evelyn's pie?"

He chuckled. "Guilty as charged."

"So you must be—"

"The doctor," Turk supplied when Lawrence hesitated. "That's right. I just opened a clinic in the Hunter's Ridge Center on Main Street."

"A doctor, huh?" Harvey said, his brown eyes sharp with interest. "I bet there's a lot of women out there chasing you."

"Harvey!"

"Well, it's true, isn't it, Turk?" he said, defending himself. "Women are looking for a good man to support them in the manner in which they want to be accustomed. Nothing wrong with that. They're the one's having babies and raising them. That's a heck of a lot easier when they have a husband who brings home a good salary."

"It takes a lot of money to raise kids," Lawrence added, straight-faced. "Do you know how much it cost to go to college nowadays? I don't know how anybody does it!"

"And what about clothes? Have you priced a pair of jeans lately? Imagine buying jeans for three or four boys who are always growing like weeds and rough-housing and tearing their clothes."

"Guys!"

Grinning at Rachel's protest, Turk only encouraged them. "And don't forget food. Can you imagine feeding three growing boys for eighteen years! And they'll want cars…and MP3s and cell phones and—"

"Speaking of children, Harvey, I thought you were going to the Texas game with your son," Rachel said smoothly, changing the subject. "Or was that next weekend?"

"No, it was today, but he had to cancel. He's got some kind of stomach bug, so he's at home in bed."

"He needs a wife like Rachel," Lawrence said. "She'd take care of him, make chicken soup for him, baby him—"

"Lawrence—"

Ignoring her warning tone, he added, "A fella can't go wrong with a woman like Rachel. Have you tasted her fried chicken?"

"No, I can't say I've had the pleasure," Turk said, giving Rachel a pointed look. "She hasn't invited me to supper."

"Then you buy the chicken and invite her to come to your house and cook it," Harvey suggested. "You can't turn him down, Rachel. What's the poor man supposed to do with raw chicken? You can at least teach him how to cook it himself."

"Now, there's an idea!"

"No!" Rachel said firmly, struggling not to laugh. "Turk and I are just neighbors! We're not dating!"

"Well, you can change that easily enough," Harvey retorted. "Ask her out, Turk. She's got a birthday coming up. Take her dancing."

"You'd better know what you're doing," Lawrence warned. "She's good. Of course, it doesn't matter if you can dance or not—all you have to do is two-step and you can hold her all night long. I know—that's what I used to do."

"Lawrence!"

"Well, I did. There's nothing wrong with that. I bet Turk's done the same thing. Haven't you, Turk?"

He shrugged, grinning. "A man's got to do what a man's got to do. So, sweetheart, when are we going dancing?"

Torn between exasperation and amusement, she rolled her eyes. "Why isn't anyone listening to me? We're not—"

"Dating," he finished for her with a laugh. "Yes, I know. So when are you going to change that?"

A customer walked up then and she jumped at the chance to wait on them. "Gotta get back to work. Goodbye, Turk. Bye, guys."

"Don't worry," Harvey said in a voice loud enough to carry to the end of the block, "She'll come around. Just give her some time."

With heat singeing her cheeks, she didn't dare look at Turk. But then again, she didn't have to. She could hear him chuckling as he walked away.

Over the course of the next week, Rachel told herself that she didn't care how much time Turk gave her, she wasn't going out with him. But the man was damn sneaky. She didn't know how he arranged it, but it seemed like every time she turned around, she was running into him. His basket nearly collided with hers at the grocery store, he was behind her in the drive-thru at the bank, and every morning, he showed up at the bakery for a doughnut and coffee before going to his clinic. And of course, the last thing she saw every night when she went to bed was the glow from his lighted windows.

Did he know he was getting to her?

She could feel herself weakening, which made

her even more determined *not* to go out with him. She just had to stand strong, she told herself. She wanted a baby, not a relationship with a man…especially a man like Turk, who could steal a woman's heart with just a wink and a grin. She didn't want her heart stolen, didn't want to fall in love again. Not with Turk, not with anyone. If she could just remember that, she'd be fine.

So she kept her distance, distracting herself as much as possible. She spent just about every evening playing poker with her grandmother and the "boys," preparing for the tournament in Austin, but it did little good, and it was all her fault. At the tournament, she couldn't concentrate—her thoughts kept drifting to Turk—and they were soundly trounced.

"I'm sorry, guys," she told them as they headed home. "I don't know what got into me. I couldn't focus."

"You know, I've heard that's a common problem in women your age," her grandmother said dryly. "It has something to do with hormones…and falling in love."

"I'm not falling in love!" she retorted. "I'm just distracted."

True, the distraction was six foot two and had the most incredible blue eyes, but no one said a word. They didn't have to. She knew exactly what they were thinking.

Frustrated, she returned home, more determined

than ever to ignore the man. But just when she thought she could hold him at bay indefinitely, he came into the bakery one morning and caught her completely off guard. "Hey, sweetheart, what are you doing Saturday? There's a charity bowl-a-thon at Oak Park Lanes to raise money for MS. I thought maybe we could go together."

She had to give him credit—he raised his voice just enough so that it carried to the far corners of the bakery. Every customer in the place sat up straighter, waiting expectantly for her to turn him down flat, just like she always did. Swallowing a curse, she wanted to kick him. Why did he keep doing this? Surely he had to know that everyone in town was talking about them—bets were being taken at Freeman's Barbershop down the street, and the latest odds were in her favor. Why couldn't he accept the fact that he was wasting his time?

"I can't," she retorted. "I'm having dinner with my grandmother. I promised I'd take her to her favorite Chinese restaurant."

"Don't you go worrying about Evelyn," Harvey said from his favorite table near the front windows. "Lawrence and I will take her to dinner. You go raise some money for MS."

Trapped, she swallowed a silent groan. So now what was she supposed to say? *No, thanks, I don't want to raise money for MS?* She'd sound like a Scrooge, and in the time it took to make another batch of doughnuts, the news would be all over town that she'd refused to participate in one of the biggest local fund-raisers of the year.

Her gaze met Turk's, and the instant she saw the wicked humor glinting in his eyes, she knew she'd been set up. The rat was aware she wouldn't be able to turn him down, and he was loving every second of it!

It would have served him right if she'd told him to stuff it, but they both knew she wouldn't do that. Left with no choice but to give in, she gave him a look that promised him she'd deal with him later, in private, and said, "Then I guess we're going bowling."

Everyone in the bakery broke into applause.

Chapter 7

The clinic was three blocks away, and Turk found himself laughing the entire way. Oh, yeah! He couldn't remember the last time he'd worked so hard to convince a woman to go out with him. He'd finally worn her down, charmed her out of her socks, make it impossible for her to resist him. And she was his! It was just a matter of time.

Don't go patting yourself on the back, goofball, his common sense drawled in his ear. *The only reason the lady agreed to anything was because you put her on the spot in front of God and everyone. A charity, Turk? C'mon! What else could she do except accept? That was brilliant...and shameless!*

"No, we don't," he snapped, shrugging off her touch when she tried to take his hand. "Don't you get it? There is no us! How many times do I have to say it before you get it? There's no us, no we. We aren't a couple, we're not dating. I hate to be ugly, but I don't know any other way to make you understand that I'm not interested in being friends or lovers with you. Leave me alone."

"I can't, sweetheart. I love you. And you'll love me, too, when you let down your guard. Now, about dinner, there must be a decent place to eat in this backward little town. Or I could cook for you," she decided, smiling in delight at the idea. "I make a fabulous lasagna. Give me the keys to your house, and I'll have everything ready by the time you get home this afternoon. Do you want to eat first thing or make love? You're tense, sweetheart. Maybe you should have a massage first. Just to help you relax—"

"No!" Cringing at the very idea of her touching him, he jerked open the door to the examining room. "Get out, Laureen. Go back to Dallas and find yourself a good psychiatrist—you need help. And the next time you decide to do something crazy and hurt yourself, go to the emergency room. Maybe someone there can help you. I can't."

In the time it took to blink, fury flashed in her eyes. "I'm not crazy!"

"I didn't say you were," he retorted. "I said you

needed help. Now, if you'll excuse me, I have other patients to see. You can pay at the front desk."

"You're the one who'll pay, Turk," she promised. "Just wait. You're going to regret speaking to me this way. I'll make sure of it."

He regretted ever speaking to her, period, not to mention asking her out, but she didn't stick around to hear that. Storming down the hall, she didn't stop to pay her bill at the billing desk, and no one tried to stop her. Jerking open the door, she swept outside without a backward glance and let the door fly.

Turk didn't flinch. She was gone. Thank God! She had to be the densest woman he'd ever met in his life. Had she gotten the message? He wanted to think she had, but who knew for sure? She hadn't paid her bill, and he wouldn't put it past her to use that as a reason to get in touch with him when he billed her. He'd nip that in the bud right now, he decided grimly. He wouldn't bill her at all.

With the matter settled, he returned to Mrs. Carson, apologizing for the delay, but he couldn't dismiss Laureen from his thoughts nearly as easily as he'd hoped. What would the crazy woman do next? Would she hurt herself again? She'd burned herself pretty badly, and while that had gotten her past the front desk, things hadn't turned out the way she'd obviously hoped. What if next time, she decided to hurt herself so severely that she ended up in the hospital? As much as he disliked her, he couldn't just ignore the fact that she was a danger to herself. There had to be something he could do.

But when he dropped by the police station after work, he quickly discovered that there wasn't much anyone could do. "She's not hurting anyone but herself," Doug Walker, a detective with the Hunter's Ridge police department, told him. "She hasn't been declared incompetent. She hasn't committed a crime. Until she breaks the law, there's nothing we can do."

"So you know she could kill herself and you do nothing?" Turk said incredulously. "That's nuts! There must be something someone can do!"

"Convince her to check herself into a mental hospital," the detective told him. "She needs help."

"Yeah, right," he snorted. "You try telling her that. When I tried to get through to her, she threatened me. I want nothing to do with the woman."

Walker frowned. "Threatened you how? If she's threatening your life, there may be something we can do about that."

"No, it wasn't that kind of threat. She was just mad when I told her she needed a psychiatrist. She stormed out of the clinic threatening to make me pay for that."

"Do you think she's capable of hurting you?"

Turk immediately started to dismiss such an idea, only to hesitate. "To be perfectly honest, I don't know her well enough to know what she's capable of. I know she's got a quick temper…and a hell of a lot of nerve. Other than that, it's hard to say what she would do."

"You can get a TRO if she keeps harassing you. Temporary restraining order," he explained when Turk lifted an inquiring brow. "And you can try to get a protective order against her, but if she has mental problems, she's going to ignore the order and do what she damn well pleases."

"And you can't really do anything until she hurts me or herself."

"Unfortunately, no," he replied. "At this point, all I can advise you to do is stay as far away from her as possible."

"Trust me—I'm trying! I moved, changed my phone numbers, and cut myself completely off from her. Three weeks later, she shows up at my clinic. I can't refuse her treatment if she's hurt."

"No, but you can give her minimum treatment and call an ambulance. If she objects and becomes disruptive, call me. We can arrest her for that."

Thanking him for the advice, Turk knew he meant well, but Laureen wasn't concerned about being arrested. He'd unintentionally insulted her, and there wasn't a doubt in his mind that she would be back. The question was…when?

Saturday was nearly a week away, and Rachel clung to the thought that surely something would come up between now and then so she wouldn't have to keep her date with Turk. But the week flew by, and before she knew it, it was Saturday. In less than an hour, he'd be knocking at her front door.

Panic twisted her stomach in knots at the thought, and she almost called him to tell him she was sick. But her pride screamed in outrage, and her common sense warned her he'd never let her get away with such a flimsy excuse. He was a doctor, for heaven's sake! Knowing him, he'd insist on coming over to check on her, and all he'd have to do was look at her to know that she was just nervous. And oh, how he'd delight in that!

Irritated, she refused to give him that kind of satisfaction. Okay, so she had no choice but to go bowling with him, but they weren't really going on a date. It was for charity. Granted, he was picking her up at her house and taking her home afterward, but there was nothing the least bit romantic about it. They weren't going to dinner or out for a drink later—she didn't even plan to wear perfume! They'd bowl two games and he'd bring her home. Big deal.

Relieved that she'd worked it all out in her head, she changed into jeans and a knit shirt. But when she stood before the full-length mirror in her bedroom, she wrinkled her nose in distaste. The jeans were slouchy and the once red shirt must have faded in the last wash. Without a thought, she turned back to her closet.

When her doorbell rang thirty minutes later, she was dressed in her best jeans and her favorite

sweater, but only because nothing else she tried on
seemed right for bowling. If her hair was soft and
feminine on her shoulders, she certainly hadn't
worn it that way because she thought it would
appeal to Turk. She just looked better with it down.
And yes, she was wearing her favorite lipstick...
because her lips were dry, and perfume—because
she loved the scent of it. She certainly wasn't trying
to attract Turk.

Satisfied that he wouldn't mistakenly think she
was actually looking forward to going out with him,
she headed for the front door. If her knees were
knocking and her heart was threatening to pound
right out of her chest, she told herself it was only
because she really didn't want to do this. Her
sudden nervousness had nothing to do with Turk.

And for a few moments, she actually believed
that. Then she opened the door to him.

"Wow!" he said, flashing her a wicked, teasing
grin. "You look great!"

Suddenly more nervous than she'd ever been in
her life, she frowned, "Don't get any ideas, Turk.
This is not a date."

"Really?" Amusement danced in his eyes. "I
really make you nervous, don't I?"

"No, of course not!"

"You're perfectly safe with me, you know. I
promise I won't kiss you in front of everyone at the
bowling alley."

"You're not kissing me, period!"

He grinned. "Wanna bet?"

Heat climbed in her cheeks. Damn the man! How could he make her laugh when she was determined not to? "No," she retorted. "You make everything a throw down, and I'm not going there with you. So behave yourself!"

"Yes, dear. Whatever you say, dear."

"I am not your dear!"

Not the least discouraged, he chuckled, "You're fighting a losing battle here. You know that, don't you? You're as attracted to me as I am to you."

"I am not!"

"Really? I'll prove it to you." And with what seemed like no effort at all, he pulled her into his arms.

Her heart was pounding long before his mouth covered hers. She expected a hot, hungry kiss, the kind that no woman in her right mind would be able to resist, but she should have known he wouldn't hit her with the obvious. Whisper-soft, he kissed her slowly, gently, with a care that was her undoing. Her thoughts clouded, her mouth moved under his, and she melted against him, kissing him back with a hunger that seemed to come from the depths of her being.

Later, she couldn't have said how long they stood there in her open doorway, kissing in front of God and anyone who happened to pass by. Lost to everything but the feelings he stirred in her so effortlessly, she could have kissed him for hours, days...

But just as his hands swept over her, turning her boneless, he reluctantly drew back, putting her gently from him before she could even begin to guess his intentions.

It wasn't until she slowly opened her eyes and her gaze met the satisfied glint in his that she realized just how much she'd told him about her feelings, all without saying a word.

Jerking back, she rasped, "A kiss doesn't prove anything—"

"The hell it doesn't, sweetheart. You kissed me back and did a darn good job of it. For a moment there, I actually thought you cared."

"Oh, *please!*" she groaned. "That was nothing but pure chemistry and you know it!"

"Aha! So you are attracted to me! You just admitted it!"

"I did not! Chemistry and attraction are two different things."

"That's okay, sweetheart, you keep telling yourself that," he said easily, taking her hand and pulling her outside with him. "We both know the truth. I understand if you have a hard time admitting it to yourself. You're one of those women who likes to win. Nothing wrong with that. We're going to burn up the lanes today! Let's go."

He linked his fingers with hers before she could stop him, and within seconds, they were walking down the street hand in hand. "What are you doing?" she demanded, tugging at her hand. "I thought we were taking the car."

"It's only four blocks to the bowling alley, and it's a beautiful day. I thought we'd walk."

She didn't have a problem with that, but holding hands? "Can I have my hand back?"

"When we get to the bowling alley," he said, chuckling. "C'mon. Relax. I don't have cooties. I promise."

Swinging their joined hands, he grinned down at her, and Rachel found herself charmed. He was impossible, she thought, swallowing a groan. And far too clever. With nothing more than a kiss and the feel of her hand in his, he made her forget that the only man she was looking for was a sperm donor.

Ten minutes later, they reached the bowling alley, and just as he promised, Turk released her hand, but only to introduce her to a dozen or more of his friends. "Hey, everybody, this is my date, Rachel Martin. Rachel, this is John and Robert. And that's Jaxon and the tall dude is Chris and…"

Stunned, Rachel hardly heard him. "These are your friends? How? You just moved here!"

"Hey, I'm a likable kind of guy," he retorted, grinning. "Ask anyone. They'll tell you."

"He works weekends at the county hospital with us," Chris, the *tall dude*, told her with a grin. "He's as crazy as we are. When he told us he was taking you bowling on your first date, we decided you needed a chaperone, so here we are. Did I mention that you're as cute as he said you were?"

"Yeah, why didn't he take you dancing instead of bowling?" one of the other guys asked, scowling. "Then we could have danced with you!"

"I claim her for my team!" a short guy at the back of the group called out suddenly. "We're going to beat the socks off you guys."

"Hey, she's my date!" Turk protested.

"Okay, so you can be on our team, too. And Robert. He's got a wicked curve," he told Rachel with a wink. "Goes right in the pocket every time!"

Two hours later, Rachel couldn't remember when she'd last had so much fun. Turk, Robert and Burt, the short one who insisted she be on his team, were darn good bowlers. But she was better. When she got a strike on her very first ball, Turk burst out laughing. "Girl, you've been holding out on me! You didn't tell me you knew how to bowl."

Grinning, she sassed, "You didn't ask."

"So what else aren't you telling me?" he teased, his blue eyes dancing. "Maybe we should talk."

Her heart stopped in her breast. If he and his friends only knew that she was looking for a kind, intelligent man to father her baby and that she didn't ever plan to see him again, they wouldn't even be speaking to her. And she couldn't say she'd blame them.

Trying not to think what they might think of

her, she forced a smile. "So what do you want to know? That I won a pie-eating contest when I was six? Or that I know how to count cards? I wouldn't advise you to play strip poker with me. You'll be the one who'll be sitting there in your birthday suit, not me."

"Whoa-ho!" Burt laughed. "I like this girl. I knew there was a reason I wanted her on my team!"

"Back off," Turk said good-naturedly. "I saw her first."

Rachel lifted a delicately arched brow at him. "Excuse me?"

"C'mon, you know it's true. I was standing in line at the bakery, just waiting my turn at coffee and doughnuts, and there you were, just daring me to ask you out."

"I was not!"

"So I did, and what did you do? Turn me down flat. But that's okay," he assured her, his blue eyes dancing with mischief. "I don't get discouraged that easily. I can beg."

"Stop that!" she laughed, blushing as his friends all started ribbing him. "I didn't make you beg. You wouldn't take no for an answer."

"Only because I knew you didn't want me to. I know when a woman wants me."

"Turk!"

"Okay, okay, time to break this party up," Burt said with a chuckle. "If you guys are going to start getting

all mushy on us, we're going to hit the road. Next time
you need twelve chaperones, call us. This was fun."

"Hey, what if we don't want to leave?" Robert
objected. "Let's bowl another game."

Six inches shorter and fifty pounds lighter, Burt
grabbed him by the scruff of the neck. "They want
to be alone, knucklehead. It's time for us to leave."

"Oh. *Ohhh!* Well, why didn't you say so? Bye,
Rachel. It was great meeting you. If you ever decide
to dump Mr. Wonderful here," he told her, nudging
Turk, "give me a call. I'm taller than he is...and
cuter. Ask my mom. She'll tell you."

"That's because she's your mother, dummy," one
of the other guys said as they all headed for the
door. "She's lied to you all these years. You just
didn't know it."

"What? No way!"

"Yeah. I'm telling you—"

Unable to stop smiling as she and Turk followed
the others outside, Rachel chuckled, hating to see
them go. "I like your friends."

"They're good guys."

"But they didn't have to run off. We're not
getting mushy."

"Sure we are," he chuckled, taking her hand.
"C'mon, I'll walk you home."

She shouldn't have let him take her hand again, but
it just felt so right. And what would it hurt? she told
herself. It was only four blocks to her house. In ten

minutes, she'd be telling him good-night and going inside, anyway. What could happen in ten minutes?

His thumb slid caressingly across her palm, making her heart skip in her breast. Just that quickly she was breathless. "Turk—"

At her warning tone, his hand tightened around hers. "Yes, sweetheart?"

Her lips twitched. "You're outrageous. You don't need to hold my hand, Doctor. I know my way home."

"So do I," he chuckled. "And I like holding your hand. It fits just perfectly in mine. Haven't you noticed?"

She had, but she wasn't about to tell him that. "I'll bet you tell all your dates that," she said dryly.

"Actually, I've never said that to anyone before," he said, sobering. "Interesting, huh?"

Interesting didn't begin to describe it, she thought, shaken. What was going on here? Why *did* her hand feel so right in his? And what was she going to do about it?

Her heart pounding at the thought, she arched a brow at him as both their houses came into view down the street. "Why aren't you married?" she asked curiously.

He grinned. "You mean because I'm cute and adorable and such a good catch? You know, I've asked myself the same thing. What's wrong with you women? Don't you know a good thing when you see it?"

"Hey, don't blame me," she retorted. "I would have thought a smart woman would have snapped you up years ago."

"Oh, they tried," he admitted ruefully. "But they didn't fit in with my career plans."

"You're never going to get married?"

"I didn't say that. I've just got my life planned out, and there's no room for a wife right now. I've got to establish my practice before I can even think about settling down with a wife and kids."

"How long do you think that'll take? Not that I'm interested for myself," she hurriedly assured him. "I'm just curious."

"No problem," he said easily. "I figure I'll need two years. The practice'll be established, and I may even have enough business to take on a partner by then."

Two years, Rachel thought. If her biological clock hadn't been ticking for some time now—and she'd been looking for a man—Turk Garrison would have been worth waiting for. And he was right. She *was* attracted to him. When he kissed her—

Don't go there, she told herself sternly. She was already thirty-five. She couldn't wait until she was thirty-seven to start trying to get pregnant. And she couldn't have an affair with the man just to get pregnant. Not when he and everyone else in town would know he was the father. From the little she knew about him, it was obvious that he was the kind of man who would do the right thing and push to marry the woman he got pregnant—even though that wasn't what he'd planned for himself. She couldn't set him up that way. It wouldn't be fair.

When they reached her house, she should have thanked him for a fun evening, then hurried inside. She definitely shouldn't have swayed toward him when he smiled into her eyes as he traced the curve of her cheek. And when he pulled her into his arms and kissed her like there was no tomorrow, she should have at least tried to keep her head. She didn't.

Chapter 8

Damn, he didn't want to let her go. Every time he held her, kissed her, felt her melt against him, all he could think of was sweeping her up in his arms and carrying her off to bed. But if he was crazy enough to do that, he had a feeling that he wouldn't surface for days, and even then, he didn't know if that would be long enough to do everything he wanted to do to the sweet, hot, willing woman in his arms.

And that would be nothing but a mistake.

She wasn't the kind of woman who had wild flings, then moved on to the next man. She was Betty Crocker, for heaven's sake! He'd watched her with her customers, with her grandmother and her friends—they all loved her. She was the kind of woman who needed a passel of kids to look after, to cook for, to love. The kind of woman who wouldn't get all bent out of shape if one of her kids tracked mud into the house or put their feet on the couch. And if she made love anything like she kissed, the man in her life would be one lucky son of a gun.

But he wasn't going there, he reminded himself. Not yet. Not for years. That didn't make it any easier to let her go. With need burning in his gut, he had to will himself to release her one finger at a time.

"Say good-night, Rachel," he rasped. "While you still can."

For a moment, he thought she was going to pull him inside with her. Dazed, her eyes dark with desire, she started to sway toward him, her hand already reaching for his. Then she blinked, and just that quickly, she came to her senses. "Good night," she said huskily. And without another word, she disappeared inside.

Later, Turk didn't remember crossing her yard to his. And he sure as hell didn't remember why he'd decided to be so damn decent and back off. As he crawled into his lonely bed and the scent of her perfume still teased his senses, all he could remember was the feel of her in his arms and the hot, hungry taste of her kiss. And he wanted her more than he'd ever wanted a woman in his life.

* * *

During the night, the first cold front of the season arrived, bringing with it cooler temperatures, a wild display of thunder and lightning, and heavy rain. By the time Rachel headed for work at four-thirty, however, the norther had moved well to the south. The streets were still wet and the trees were dripping, but there was nothing she loved more than walking to work after a storm. Dawn wasn't even a promise on the horizon, and the damp quiet of the morning called to her soul.

Not surprisingly, the streets were deserted and she had Hunter's Ridge all to herself. And she loved it. The display windows of the antiques stores on Main Street were lit with tiny white lights that twinkled like jewels in the predawn darkness. As she made her way to the bakery, she stopped for a second at the Moment in Time antique store to study the new display of antique kitchen bowls and old-fashioned utensils she would love to have on display at the bakery. Maybe she'd come by after work.

Already planning where she would put the bowls as she continued toward the bakery, she never saw the car turn onto Main Street two blocks behind her. It picked up speed and was almost upon her when she suddenly realized she was no longer alone. Surprised, she glanced over her shoulder and frowned at the sight of the black SUV heading down the street toward her.

It wasn't often that she saw anyone other than someone from the police or sheriff's department on the streets at that hour of the morning. And whoever was behind the wheel of the SUV was moving fast. Already fifty feet away, they were racing down the street at a reckless speed that was more than a little alarming.

Was the driver drunk? she wondered, concerned. Suddenly aware of just how deserted the streets were, she felt her heart jump into her throat and tried to convince herself that she was perfectly safe. Then the SUV headed straight for her.

It happened so fast, she didn't have time to scream. Her heart slammed against her ribs, the headlights trapped her in the early-morning darkness, and her feet were suddenly nailed to the ground.

"Move!" a voice in her head screamed. Dazed, she would have sworn she couldn't. But suddenly, the SUV was bearing down on her like the devil himself, and with a cry of horror, she turned to run, only to slip on the wet sidewalk and turn her ankle painfully. Still, she scrambled for purchase. Sobbing, she could have sworn she felt the heat of the engine on her back, but before she could jump out of the way, her feet flew out from under her and she hit the wet sidewalk with a jarring thud.

Pain shot up her spine. Glancing wildly over her shoulder, she could see nothing but the black monster of a truck as it jumped the curb and headed straight for her. Later, she knew she must have screamed. A split second later, the SUV swerved back onto the street and hit a puddle, dousing her to the skin. She only had time to gasp before the vehicle raced around the next corner and disappeared from view.

Later, she couldn't have said how long she lay there, her blood roaring in her ears, gasping for breath. Too close! she thought, shaken. Dear God, that was too damn close! All she could think of was that she would have been dead if the driver, for whatever reason, hadn't decided to swerve around her.

And just that quickly, she was livid. Idiot! Jackass! What kind of nutcase played chicken on Main Street when the roads were slick? Did he realize how close he'd come to killing her? Did he even care? She had to call the police, had to—

Suddenly realizing she was soaked to the skin, she gasped. How could she go to work looking like this? She was a mess! She was dripping wet, her right ankle throbbed so painfully that she could hardly push to her feet, and she'd never been so angry in her life. Jackass! Was he drunk or just an idiot who got his kicks running down whoever happened to be on the streets when he decided to drive like a maniac? She had to call the police. Dammit, why hadn't she thought to get his license number?

Maybe because he was trying to kill you at the

time, the voice in her head retorted. *Or did you think this was just an accident?*

Still fuming, she immediately dismissed the idea that anyone would try to kill her. It was just a sick joke, a hair-raising prank. But what if it wasn't? She needed to call the police.

And tell them what? That someone almost ran you down? You don't even know the make and model of the pickup, let alone the color!

She couldn't argue with that, but the incident still needed to be reported.

Grabbing her cell phone, she quickly called the police station, then put in a call to the bakery to let Jenny, Sissy and Mick know that she was running late.

He dreamed about the woman all night.

Pulling open the front door to the bakery, Turk couldn't wait to see her. When her eyes met his, would she remember the kiss they'd shared? Would she act as if nothing happened between them? If she did, he swore he was going to step behind the counter and lay a kiss on her that would have the entire town buzzing by lunchtime.

Grinning at the thought—he could just see her, flashing those beautiful blue eyes of hers at him, making him laugh—he moved to the end of the line queued up in front of the counter. But when he looked past the crowd in front of him for Rachel, she was nowhere in sight.

Surprised, he frowned. For the past month, he'd stopped at the bakery every morning for coffee and doughnuts. And every morning, Rachel had been in the same spot, standing behind the counter, talking and laughing with her customers. The place didn't look the same without her. Where the heck was she?

He had to wait until it was his turn to order to find out. "Oh, she had an accident on the way to work," Jenny told him. "She should be coming in any second."

"Accident? Is she hurt? What happened?"

"She didn't give me the details, just that she got splashed by a car and had to go home to change. I thought she'd be here by now."

Not liking the sound of that, he frowned. "I think I'll go check on her. Let me have two coffees and her favorite doughnuts to go."

When he started to pay, Jenny waved him off with a smile. "It's for the boss. It's on the house."

Loaded down with two large coffees and a half-dozen still-hot doughnuts dripping in glaze, Turk made the walk to Rachel's house in record time. He half expected to meet her along the way, but there was no sign of her, and as the morning sky began to lighten, her house was dark when he strode up onto her front porch. Concerned—where the heck was she?—he punched the doorbell, then waited impatiently for her to answer the door.

Long minutes passed—the house was quite as a

tomb. He was starting to get seriously worried when the light in the entry hall came on. Through the frosted window of the front door, he could just make out her silhouette as she slowly made her way toward him.

"Rachel? It's me...Turk. Are you okay?" he called through the door. "Jenny said you were splashed by a car."

"I'm fine," she assured him, pulling open the door. "Well, sort of."

He took one look at her pale face and immediately stepped forward in concern. "You're white as a ghost! What's wrong? You're hurt!" he said accusingly when she stepped back, clutching her fuzzy robe closed, and winced. Swearing, he swept her up into his arms. "What the hell have you done to yourself?"

"I haven't done anything," she retorted. "Some idiot nearly ran me down on Main Street. When I jumped out of the way, I twisted my ankle. I'm fine, Turk. It's just a sprain."

"I'm the doctor," he growled. "I'll be the judge of that."

Carrying her into the living room, he gently set her on the overstuffed couch, then dropped down on a knee in front of her to exam her left ankle. Before he even touched her, she stiffened. "C'mon, sweetheart," he said reproachfully. "Surely you know I'm not going to hurt you."

"It's not you," she said defensively. "It just hurts."

"I know, honey. I'll be gentle. I promise."

Easing off her slip-on house shoe, he cradled her foot against his thigh, then began to examine her ankle with a touch that was whisper-soft. Braced for a stab of pain, she released her breath in a sigh. "It's just a sprain—"

"Yes, Doctor, it is," he said with a slight smile as he ran his fingers over the delicate bones of her ankle in what could only be described as a caress. "And I want you to stay off of it the rest of the day."

"The rest of the day? You can't be serious!"

"Walking on it's only going to make it worse," he said, sobering. He frowned. "Did you call the police?"

"Yes, Doctor, I did, and I filed a report."

"And what did they say?"

"Exactly what I thought they'd say. Without witnesses or a license plate number—which I didn't get—there's nothing I can do."

He swore, not surprised. "Just be careful, okay? And follow doctor's orders—stay off that foot the rest of the day."

"But I have to work! The bakery—"

"Is open for business right this minute and doing fine," he assured her. "Oh, I almost forgot. I brought you breakfast." He handed her a warm doughnut and her coffee. "As soon as you finish that, I'll carry you to bed."

"Turk!"

"Quit worrying. Jenny, Mick and Sissy had everything under control. I'm sure they can handle things. What would they do if you were in the hospital or had the flu or something?"

"They'd make do, of course. But I'm not in the hospital—"

When he just looked at her, she didn't know if she wanted to laugh or cry. This wasn't fair! "Can't you just wrap it or something?"

"I'm going to," he assured her. "I just have to go next door to get my bag. Then I'll carry you to bed."

"Carry me? But—"

A crooked grin curled his mouth. "How else are you going to get to bed, sweetcakes? You're supposed to stay off the ankle."

Leaving her with that to think about, he left her on the couch and returned five minutes later with his medical bag. Seconds later, he neatly wrapped her ankle, gave her two ibuprofen, then gently lifted her into his arms.

Her heart pounding, fighting the need to wrap her arms around his neck and kiss him senseless, she said huskily, "What are you going to do? Stand guard over me all day to make sure I follow doctor's orders?"

"Something like that," he chuckled.

"But don't have you to be at the clinic?"

"Yes. But that doesn't mean I can't check in on you during the day. I'll bring you lunch," he promised.

If she'd had any sense, she would have told him that wasn't necessary—her grandmother would be happy to bring her something to eat later. But she couldn't find the words when she was held so close in his arms. With his mouth just inches from hers, all she could think about was last night...and kissing him. He'd walked in and out of her dreams all night, teasing her, seducing her, showing her just how wonderful it could be between them if she'd only drop her guard, and it was driving her crazy.

For no other reason than that, she should have thanked him for the offer and sent him packing. She wasn't sick; she didn't need a babysitter. But she was already in trouble. She was in his arms and she couldn't resist the chance to spend more time with him. He wanted to take care of her. What would it hurt just this once?

"Well," she said huskily. "If that's what you want to do."

"Good," he growled. "Then it's settled."

Starting down the hall, he carried her to her bedroom and eased her onto the mattress with a gentleness that threatened to bring tears to her eyes. "Sleep," he ordered gruffly as he pulled the covers over her, then dropped a kiss on her forehead. "I'll be back later to check on you."

"Take my keys," she told him as she laid back with a sigh, "then you can lock the front door. They're on the table in the entry hall."

"Keep that ankle elevated," he cautioned. "And call me if you need me."

He was gone before she could do anything but
nod, and as she heard him lock the front door, she
didn't think she'd ever be able to sleep. Not when
her head was in a whirl and she could still feel his
arms around her. But when she relaxed into her
pillow and closed her eyes, the trauma of the
morning caught up with her. She was asleep almost
immediately.

The sound of the key in the front door woke her
hours later. Startled, she tried to remember why she
was in bed at twelve o'clock on a workday, and
suddenly, the image of the black SUV bearing down
on her flashed through her mind. In the span of a
heartbeat, she was suddenly terrified.

"Who's there?" she called sharply.

"It's me…Turk."

Relieved, she sighed, "Thank God! I just had the
most horrible dream about this morning."

The words were hardly out of her mouth when he
appeared at the threshold to her bedroom and studied
her with a frown. "How's the ankle?" he asked.

"Much better," she replied, and pulled the covers
aside so he could see her bare foot. "See…no
swelling. In fact," she added with a grin as she
rotated her foot, "it feels like its old self. I should
go back to work."

"Oh, no you don't," he warned, striding across
the room to sit on the end of the bed and gently
capture the foot she waved at him. "You're staying

right where you are until I check you out and make sure you're really all right."

"I'm fine—"

"Then this shouldn't bother you a bit," he countered easily, grinning, and captured her foot in both hands.

She expected him to carefully rotate her foot to test for pain, and instinctively, she braced herself. His fingers slid over her instep, tracing the arch with fingers that seemed to drag liquid fire in their wake.

Her breath catching in her throat, she couldn't take her eyes off his hands. "What are you doing?" she asked huskily.

He smiled slightly, his eyes warm with an emotion that heated her stomach. "Playing footsie. Wanna play?"

"Turk—"

"Just keep saying my name like that, sweetheart."

"We can't do this."

His hand slid slowly up her calf. "Why not?"

She couldn't, for the life of her, think of a single reason. Not when he was melting her bones one by one and he hadn't done anything but trail his fingers from the arch of her foot to the curve of her calf to the inside of her knee. Who knew that spot behind her knee could be so incredibly sensitive?

Desperately wishing he would kiss her, she moaned, "You don't play fair."

"I'll stop…if you really want me to."

He wouldn't, she thought, aching. But then he

started to pull his hand away from her knee. "No!" Lightning quick, she caught his hand…and pulled him onto the bed with her…and into her arms. "Nobody said anything about stopping," she told him when he grinned. "So don't even think about going there."

"I thought you said we couldn't do this?" he teased.

"What?" she asked innocently, rubbing her bare foot up and down his calf. "Play footsie?"

"Witch," he groaned, and kissed her.

It wasn't until his mouth covered hers, claiming her, seducing her, that she realized that she'd been waiting ever since last night for him to kiss her again. Moaning softly, she kissed him as the pounding of her heart drowned out the warning bells clanging in her head.

"Your ankle…?" he groaned against her mouth, suddenly remembering. "Damn! I forgot! Tell me it's not hurting you. Don't make me beg. Because if you're feeling even a twinge of pain, we're not doing this."

He sounded so tortured that she had to laugh. "It's fine. Really," she said when he looked skeptical. Unbuttoning his shirt, she spread it open and slowly slid her hands over his chest. Seconds later, her mouth followed her hands. Smiling as she kissed the side of his neck and felt him groan, she murmured, "I do have this ache, though…."

"Really? Then I guess I'll have to see what I can

do about that. Where does it ache? Here? How about here?"

"Oh, yes!"

With nothing more than a touch, he had her arching under him, his name a cry of pleasure on her lips, and there was no more time for teasing. Their clothes disappeared, their blood heated, and the world outside her bedroom ceased to exist. There was only the two of them, driving each other crazy with the slow glide of a hand, a mouth, a tongue.

On the verge of losing all reason, Rachel struggled to hang on to her common sense. She couldn't let him make love to her without a condom. As much as she wanted a baby—and the timing couldn't have been more perfect for her to get pregnant!—she couldn't bring herself to use Turk that way.

And that's when she knew she was in serious trouble. He didn't want to settle down and get married and have children for years...and that had nothing to do with her. So why was she putting her hopes and dreams on hold for him?

She should have stopped him right then, used the excuse that her ankle was hurting her and apologized for waiting so long to tell him. But she couldn't. Not when she wanted him so badly. "You have a condom, don't you?" she asked huskily, fighting the sudden need to cry. What was wrong with her?

"Don't worry, sweetheart. I'll protect you," he

promised, reaching for his wallet. "Now, where were we?"

Even as he asked, he knew. They were in the middle of something damn hot, something so intense that he'd have completely forgotten about protection if she hadn't. And it was all her fault. After all this time, she was finally in his arms, and he readily admitted that no woman had ever tied him in knots quite the way she did. There was something about her skin, the soft beauty of her breasts, the way she filled his arms as if she were made for him. And when she took him deep, he was hers.

He wanted her desperate for him, but he was the one who felt desire sink its claws into him. She moved under him...and made him burn. A groan ripped from his throat. Then she softly moaned his name, her breathless whisper calling to the deepest part of his soul, and what was left of his control snapped. Moving with her, in her, he drove them both to the edge of reason...and over.

She was so close to falling in love with him that her heart ached with it.

Pacing the confines of her bedroom long after he'd returned to his clinic, Rachel tried to tell herself she was imagining things. She was just confusing sex with love.

But she knew better. She'd been in love, and she knew what it felt like. And she wasn't going there again. It had nothing to do with Turk. He was nothing like her ex…except that she'd thought her ex was wonderful when she'd fallen in love with him, too. Then, when he finally told her he'd had a vasectomy a week before they got married, she realized that she'd never really known the man she promised to spend her life with.

She wasn't making that mistake again. She couldn't. She wasn't getting married again, wasn't putting her trust in another man. Even if that man did make her bones melt and her heart pound. She just couldn't take that kind of chance. Because if he turned out not to be the man she thought he was, she didn't think she'd be able to bear it.

The phone rang then, startling her, and she hesitated. If that was Turk, she couldn't talk to him. Not now. Not when she wanted to run to him and from him at one and the same time. She couldn't see him again, couldn't make love to him again, couldn't chance losing her heart to him. It would just hurt too much.

The phone rang for the fourth time—and the answering machine kicked on. "Rachel? It's me? Are you there? Pick up."

At the sound of her best friend's voice, Rachel wilted in relief. "Hi, Sandy. What's going on?"

"What's today?"

Rachel frowned. "I don't know…Tuesday? The…what? Fifteenth? Sixteenth? Oh, my God, it's your birthday!"

"Got it in one! The big four-O."

"I'm so sorry! I should have called. Things have been crazy, but that's no excuse. So how does it feel?"

"Like somebody died!" she groaned. "I need to go out tonight, to go dancing, to feel young again! Wanna go with me? I don't want to go alone."

Caught off guard, Rachel cringed at the thought. She didn't want to go out, didn't want to deal with the smoke and the flirts and the whole scene. But she and Sandy had been friends forever, and she was right— she shouldn't go out alone on her fortieth birthday.

"Sure, I'll go," she said, trying to infuse some enthusiasm into her voice. "I'll be designated driver. What time do you want me to pick you up?"

"Six," she said promptly. "We'll go eat first. How does the Bayou sound?"

"Expensive," Rachel laughed. "But you don't turn forty every day, so it'll be my treat."

"Oh, no! I didn't mean for you to—"

"I know. I want to. On my fortieth, you can return the favor."

"There you go, rubbing it in that you're younger," Sandy teased. "You could at least look your age! You're thirty-five, for heaven's sake! When are you going to look it?"

"Ask my grandmother," she laughed. "She still doesn't look her age and she's going to be eighty in August! Some of us just have good genes."

"And some of us don't," she grumbled. "Maybe I should look into Botox."

"Don't you dare! You're beautiful the way you are. I'll see you at six."

Still smiling when she hung up, Rachel turned to her closet. What was she going to wear to the Bayou?

Chapter 9

Fighting the need to call her after work, Turk told himself to give the lady…and himself…some space. He was still reeling from the loving they'd shared earlier in the day. And he didn't mind admitting that that scared the hell out of him. He'd thought of nothing but her all afternoon. The heat of her, the silky softness, the taste of her. And it was driving him crazy. How had she done it? How had she gotten under his skin so easily? And what the heck was he going to do about it?

He needed to go out, clear his head, maybe play some pool and just forget about the woman for a while. There was a new place that had just opened between Hunter's Ridge and Austin that was drawing big crowds. Maybe he'd check it out.

But first he had to go home and change.

Yeah, right, that irritating voice in his head mocked. *You don't need to go home to change. You want to go next door and check on Rachel.*

Swearing, he couldn't deny it. He was going to check on her, just to make sure she wasn't having any more problems with her ankle, and then he'd leave. It'd take all of thirty seconds.

Confident he could walk away from her with no trouble, he pulled into his own driveway, only to swear when he saw that her car was gone. So much for checking on her, he thought with a scowl. If she felt well enough to drive, there obviously wasn't a damn thing wrong with her ankle.

So why the hell was he suddenly so irritated? he wondered as he strode into his house to change. He should have been relieved. If she'd been home and he'd gotten within touching distance of her, he'd have been hard pressed to keep his hands off her. And he'd sworn he was going to back off, dammit! She'd just made it easy for him. So why was he still here? He had a game of pool waiting for him.

Dinner was fantastic—and Rachel had to force herself to eat it. She shouldn't have come, she decided grimly. She really wasn't in the mood. Every time she let her guard down, her thoughts wandered to Turk. Had he come by to check her ankle again? He'd said he might. She should have called him and told him she was going out—

Frowning at the direction of her thoughts, she stiffened. What was wrong with her? She and Turk weren't dating. There was no commitment between them—she wasn't making the mistake of acting as if there was. She didn't report to the man just because they'd made love.

And it wasn't love! she told herself fiercely. Sex. That's all it was. As much as that offended the romantic in her soul, she refused to consider the possibility that what they'd shared could be anything else.

"So I told him the next time he decided to buy drugs on the street, he could use his own money."

Caught up in her musings, Rachel only just then heard what Sandy said. "What?"

She grinned. "So I finally got your attention. Where've you been? What's his name?"

Heat spilled into her cheeks. "I don't know what you're talking about."

"Of course you do. But that's okay—you don't have to tell me about him until you're ready."

Thankful she hadn't pushed her to tell her more, she arched a brow at her. "So where are we going now?"

"There's this new country-western place…"

Rachel winced. "Country-western? C'mon,

Sandy, look how we're dressed! We can't go to a place like that dressed like we're going to the symphony or something."

"What?" she asked, frowning down at her black lace cocktail dress. "This old thing? Nobody's going to look twice at me in this."

Grinning, Rachel knew better. "Nice try, but you could wear your grandmother's flannel nightgown and stop traffic and you know it."

Her green eyes danced with mischief. "Then just think what I can do dressed like this. Let's go."

Just as Rachel had predicted, they drew the eye of every man in the place when they walked into McCall's Saloon and Dance Hall fifteen minutes later. Thirty seconds later, Sandy was on the dance floor with a tall, dark-haired cowboy with a wicked grin. Left to her own devices, Rachel made her way to the bar. Before she'd even climbed onto a bar stool, two different men asked her to dance. With the irony of the situation not lost on her, she politely but firmly turned them down flat. All this time, when she'd been going to bars around the medical center, hoping to find a suitable father for the baby she hoped to have, she hadn't once stood out in a crowd the way she did tonight. If she'd known over-dressing was all she had to do to get the attention of just about every man in the bar, she would have done it weeks ago!

Now's your chance. There's bound to be a smart, caring, kind man somewhere in the crowd who can give you a baby...if you still want one.

She winced. Of course she still wanted a baby... so badly that just thinking about it made her want to cry. But as much as she longed to feel her own child growing inside her, she knew she was never going to get pregnant by a man she didn't even know. She didn't know why she'd ever thought she could go through with such a thing, but everything had changed when she and Turk—

"There you are! I've been looking all over for you. C'mon, let's dance."

Blinking in surprise at the man grinning at her as if they'd known each other for years, she frowned. "I'm sorry, but do I know you?"

"Not yet, but that's just a technicality," he retorted, winking at her. "We were married in another life. Don't you remember? You were Josephine and—"

"Let me guess," she stopped him, laughing, "you were the little man himself."

"I'm not surprised you didn't recognize me right away," he replied. "I'm taller this time around. I like it."

Stepping through the saloon's front door, Turk took a second for his eyes to adjust to the shadowy lighting, then headed for the bar for a beer. He'd taken only three steps, however, when his gaze fell on a woman flirting with a man at the far end of the bar.

Rachel.

She was with another man.

Stunned, he stopped short. This didn't make sense. Rachel wasn't the type of woman who would make love with one man in the afternoon, then go out with a different one in the evening. Granted, he hadn't known her all that long, but he'd seen her with her friends and family and customers, and he would have sworn she had more principles than that.

His eyes, however, weren't deceiving him, he acknowledged grimly as his gaze skirted to the Casanova grinning at Rachel with lust in his eyes. The jackass wanted her. And from the smile on her face, she was thoroughly enjoying his company.

Until that moment in time, Turk had never considered himself a jealous man. But just watching Rachel smile at another man really chapped his hide. It would serve her right if he stormed over to her and the jerk monopolizing her and demanded to know what the hell she thought she was doing. But he wouldn't, by God! He'd be damned if he'd act like a Neanderthal, especially when they weren't even dating!

For all of two seconds, he gave serious consideration to leaving. But he'd come there for a beer and a game of pool, and by God, nothing was getting in the way of that...especially a woman who thought so little of him and what they'd shared that afternoon that she'd almost immediately gone out with someone else!

His face set in hard, unyielding lines, he turned away, determined to not even look in her direction again.

Fate, however, had other ideas. Before he could take a single step, Rachel looked up and saw him glaring at her. A blind man couldn't have missed the shock that flared in her eyes. Cursing, Turk stepped over to the bar and curtly ordered a beer.

He didn't look her way again, but he wasn't surprised when she joined him a few minutes later. She wasn't the kind of woman who would duck her head and run from anything or anyone. "We need to talk," she said quietly.

He didn't spare her a glance. "I have nothing to say to you. Go back to your date."

"He's not my date," she retorted. "Dammit, Turk, will you look at me? I'm here with a friend."

"Yeah, right," he sneered. "I saw him."

Rachel wanted to shake him. The second her eyes had met his and she saw his face turn to stone, she'd known he'd jumped to all the wrong conclusions. "My friend, Sandy, turned forty today," she told his back. "She wanted to celebrate. She's the blonde in the black lace dress on the dance floor.

"You don't owe me any explanations—"

"Maybe not," she replied, "but I'm giving you one, anyway. I don't want any misunderstandings between us."

He laughed sarcastically. "Oh, yeah, it's crystal clear." Nodding toward the man watching her every move from the far end of the bar, he said, "Tell Sandy I said hi."

His words struck her like a slap, and she felt the sting all the way to her soul. He didn't believe her. Why did that hurt so badly? "His name's not Sandy! To be perfectly honest, I don't know what it is, and I don't care. But you're not going to believe me, so what's the point of talking about it, right?"

She was going home. Turning her back on him, she hugged herself, searching the dance floor for Sandy. She didn't have to look far. Right at that moment, her friend rushed up with a huge smile on her face, tugging a tall cowboy behind her. "Look who's here, Rachel! You remember Jack Scott, don't you? He and my brother were roommates in college. We thought we'd go somewhere quiet and catch up on old times. Want to go with us?"

Fighting the need to cry, she forced a smile. "Actually, I'd rather not, if you don't mind. If Jack can take you home, I think I'll call it a night. I've got a headache."

Immediately concerned, Sandy frowned. "Why didn't you say so? I'll drive you home." Glancing over her shoulder at Jack, she said, "You don't mind, do you, Jack? I'll call you tomorrow."

"Don't be ridiculous," Rachel said. "I can drive myself home. I'll be fine. You two have a good time. I'll call you tomorrow, Sandy."

She walked out without a backward look and never heard Turk swear. She *was* with a friend. Dammit! It had taken him weeks to talk her into going out with him, and even longer to get her into bed, and he'd just ruined it all. Infuriated with himself, he bit off a curse. He wouldn't blame her if she never spoke to him again. It was no more than he deserved.

He had to find a way to make this up to her, he thought grimly. And the only way to start was with an apology, the sooner, the better. His jaw set at a determined angle, he strode out after her, but by the time he reached the parking lot, she was already gone. His shoulders slumping, he dropped his head and swore. Damn.

Her house was dark, her driveway empty, when he pulled into his own driveway fifteen minutes later. Concerned, he frowned. She should have easily beat him home…unless she had some kind of car trouble. Frowning at the thought, he considered the possibility, only to dismiss it. She would have taken the same route he had—it was the only way home—and he'd have seen her if she'd had some kind of breakdown. She'd probably gone for a drive, instead, to clear the cobwebs out of her head. She'd be home in a little while. In the meantime, he had to find a way to make up for his stupidity. Where could he get roses at ten o'clock at night?

It was almost eleven when Rachel finally went home. She'd spent the past hour at the bakery, working on a new pie recipe to enter in the county fair next month, but she hadn't gotten very far. And it was all Turk's fault. He kept pushing his way into her thoughts, making it next to impossible for her to concentrate. How could he accuse her of being there with another man? Did he really think she would go out with someone else just hours after she'd made love with him? What kind of woman did he think she was?

I wouldn't go there if I were you. Remember that doctor you've been looking for? The kind, caring one you were looking for to give you a baby? How do you think Turk would feel about you if he found out about that?

Pulling into her driveway, she cringed at the thought. Okay, so she wasn't an angel. For a while there, she'd gotten caught up in the panic of never having a baby and she'd almost done something stupid. Everyone made mistakes. Thankfully, she'd come to her senses.

That didn't mean she no longer worried about her biological clock running out, she thought as she started up the front walk. She'd just realized that she wasn't so desperate that she'd do anything to have a baby.

Caught up in her thoughts, she stepped onto her front porch…and almost tripped over the large rose bush blocking her front door. Planted in a five-gallon bucket, the three yellow roses that clung to the plant were turning brown and more than a little the worse for wear. "What the—"

"I couldn't find a florist that was open so I dug up the rose bush in my backyard," Turk said gruffly from the deep shadows of the porch. "I acted like a jackass. I'm sorry."

Stunned, Rachel couldn't believe she'd heard him correctly. "You dug up your rose bush for me?"

"I had to find some way to apologize," he said simply. "I treated you like dirt. I wouldn't blame you if you never spoke to me again."

She winced. "You don't have to do this—"

"Yes, I do," he insisted. "I don't know what possessed me to talk to you that way. I guess I was jealous. I saw you laughing and talking with that cowboy after we'd—"

"I understand, Turk…"

"Then you're doing better than I am," he retorted with a wry grimace. "Because I don't understand any of this—except that I was a jerk. You should have slapped me. But you're not that kind of woman. I know that."

Feeling guiltier by the second, Rachel couldn't let him continue to castigate himself. "Don't do this, Turk. We all have our moments when we do stuff we wish we hadn't. Don't beat yourself up over it."

"Yeah, right. Easy for you to say. What have you ever done that's so terrible? Short-changed one of your customers by accident?"

"No." She hesitated but she knew if she didn't tell him now she never could. "I decided I wanted a baby, so I prowled the bars in Austin, looking for a stranger to father my child."

The words hung in the air between them like the sharp blade of a guillotine, waiting to fall. "Oh, c'mon, you did not!"

If she'd have denied it then, she knew she could have made him believe her. But guilt was weighing on her, consuming her, and after the tender, incredible way he'd made love to her, she knew she couldn't lie to him anymore. If he hadn't lived next door to her when she'd come up with her crazy idea to get pregnant by a stranger, she would have plotted and schemed to seduce him because he was just the type of man she'd wanted to father her baby... smart, kind, funny, intelligent.

"Yes, I did," she said quietly. "I wanted a baby. I just didn't want a man to go with it anymore."

She didn't want to tell him the rest, but she was in too deep. After he thought about it, she knew he would figure out the rest of the story. "My friends wanted me to go to a sperm bank," she continued, "but I didn't want that. It was too impersonal. So I decided what kind of man I wanted the father of my baby to be, then I went looking for him."

"Where?" he growled, scowling. "How'd you know where to find this paragon of virtue?"

Trapped, she knew she would lose whatever friendship she had with him right then and there if she told him the truth, but her conscience would let her do nothing less. "The bars around the medical center," she said simply.

For a moment, he didn't make the connection. "Bars around the medical center—"

Then her meaning registered. In the blink of an eye, the light in his eyes flashed from surprise to red-hot anger. "A doctor? You were looking for a doctor to father your baby?"

He was furious. And the betrayal in his eyes struck her right in the heart. "I wanted the father of my baby to be kind and caring and intelligent. I would hope that a doctor would have all those qualities, but being an M.D. wasn't a requirement. I just figured I had a better chance of getting what I wanted with a doctor."

Still reeling, he had a hard time wrapping his brain around the fact that she was so conniving, and he'd never had a clue. How could he have been so naive? He'd seen the dollar signs in women's eyes when they looked at him and learned he was a doctor—he knew a gold digger when he saw one. He'd never seen that look in Rachel's eyes. Instead, she'd done everything she could to discourage him.

And that had only made him want her more.

Suddenly furious all over again—damn, she was manipulating!—he growled, "And I moved in right next door. Talk about dumb luck! You must have been in hog heaven."

"It wasn't like that, Turk—"

"I've got to give you credit. You were damn clever. *Do you have protection, Turk?* What the hell was that? A trick to pull me into your web so I wouldn't suspect what you were up to?"

"No—"

"Oh, c'mon," he jeered. "We both know that's exactly what you were doing. So when did you plan to tell me we didn't need a condom? When the timing was right to get pregnant?"

"No—"

"How's the timing now?" he growled. "Hell, let's just do it now and see if you hit the jackpot. That's what it's all about, isn't it? You and what you want? Gotta get you that baby. Well, c'mon, sweetheart. Let's get at it."

Before she could do anything but gasp, he grabbed her and hauled her into his arms. Pain squeezing her heart, she should have pushed free and told him exactly what she thought of him. But he was right, dammit! She hadn't cared two cents about his wishes—all she'd been able to think about was the fact that her biological clock was ticking and the older she got, the less chance she had of having a healthy baby. It *was* all about her. He had every right to despise her.

Her heart breaking—God, what had she done?—she couldn't stop the tears from welling in her eyes and spilling over. She never said a word, never fought to push him away, but she didn't have to. The second he tasted her tears, he jerked back as if he'd been scalded.

His cheeks flushed, and emotions churning in his eyes, he swore. "I never kissed a woman in anger in my life," he rasped. "I apolo—"

"Don't!" she cried. "I did this, not you. I apologize. You don't know how much I regret it—"

"Save it," he growled. "I know who you are now. There's nothing more to say. Have a nice life."

Stepping off the porch, he strode across her yard to his own without another word, and Rachel could do nothing but stand there and watch. Every instinct she had told her to go after him, to make him listen to her until he understood something she didn't even understand herself. But her feet never moved. He was in no mood to listen to her. She didn't know if he ever would be again.

Pain squeezed her heart at the thought. Stunned, she sank down onto the wooden bench where Turk had been sitting when she walked up. When had she let down her guard? she wondered. When had she forgotten how much Jason had hurt her and opened herself up to caring for another man? This wasn't supposed to happen! She wanted a baby... just a baby! Or at least, that's what she'd thought she wanted. But everything had changed the second she looked into his laughing blue eyes. And now she'd ruined it all. How in the world was she going to fix it?

When she finally went to bed at one o'clock, she still didn't have any answers. And that devastated her. What was she going to do?

Later, she couldn't have said when she fell asleep. One minute she was crying her eyes out, and the next, the phone was ringing and it was three in the morning. Startled, alarmed, she knew only one person who would call her at that hour of the night. Her heart in her throat, she snatched up the phone. "Gran? What is it? What's wrong?"

"The bakery's on fire!"

"*What?* Oh, God! I'll be right there!"

She never remembered hanging up, never remembered reaching for her robe. Seconds later, she was running down the street even as the sound of sirens ripped through the silence of the night.

Turk woke at the first sound at sirens, instantly alert. Ambulance? Fire truck? Not sure, all he could say for sure was that the vehicle was close...damn close. And someone probably needed his help. Throwing off the covers, he reached for his pants.

When he rushed outside a few minutes later with his medical bag in his hand, it took him only an instant to realize that the sirens were not only close, they sounded as if they were right around the corner on Main Street…near Rachel's bakery. Swearing, he started to run.

Even as he sprinted around the corner, he could see the smoke pouring out of the attic of the hundred-year-old building that housed the bakery. Two fire trucks were parked at the curb, pouring water onto the building, and a short distance away, an ambulance sat, ready for anything. Red and white lights whirled, and in the darkness of the night, residents of nearby homes drifted out of the edges of darkness, silently watching the unfolding scene.

Rachel…where the hell was Rachel? he wondered wildly, searching through the growing crowd for her. She had to be there. She must have heard the sirens. The second she heard them, she would have come running when she realized how close they were to the bakery and her grandmother. But there was no sign of her, and that scared the hell out of him. She wouldn't have gone inside….

He didn't even want to consider the possibility, but the bakery was her pride and joy, her baby. If she got to the fire before the fire department, he couldn't see her just standing at the curb, wringing her hands, while the place burned to the ground. She would have rushed inside without even thinking about it.

Sick at the thought, he pushed his way through the crowd toward the barrier the police had hastily assembled. He had to get inside, he thought, fighting panic. Had to find her. If she was hurt—

He was on the verge of pushing aside the wooden sawhorse barrier that stood between him and the bakery when he suddenly spied Rachel standing on the curb across the street. She had her arm around her grandmother's shoulders and was pale as a ghost. Her eyes stark with devastation, she was totally unaware of anything but the fire.

He hadn't forgotten what kind of woman she was—the argument they'd had earlier in the evening was still fresh in his mind—but none of that seemed important now. Not when she was hurting like this.

He never remembered crossing to her, but suddenly he was standing right in front of her. "Are you all right?"

She blinked, and only then brought him into focus. Immediately, tears welled in her eyes. "Oh, Turk!"

"Things aren't always as bad as they seem," he assured her huskily. "And luckily, the fire department's close. It looks like they caught it early. Do you know who called it in?"

"I did," her grandmother said, never taking her eyes from the smoke still billowing from the business she'd started all by herself, decades ago.

"I got up to go to the bathroom and I smelled the smoke. I thought it might be that little Mexican restaurant around the corner—I know they've been having problems with the wiring. But then I looked out the window and saw the smoke pouring out of the bakery. I—"

Her voice broke, and right before Turk's eyes, she seemed to crumble. Swearing, he moved lightning quick to catch her. "Whoa, sweetheart! None of that! Let's get you out of here."

"Gran!" Alarmed, Rachel stepped to his side. "We need to get her home—"

"No!" Evelyn cried. "Not until the fire's out."

"It'll only take a minute to check you out," Turk told her. "As soon as I'm sure there's nothing seriously wrong, you can come back."

He didn't give her a chance to argue but simply carried her the short distance home. Clutching his medical bag, which he'd dropped when he'd jumped to catch her grandmother, Rachel hurried to open the front door for him.

"I'm all right!" Evelyn insisted when he gently laid her on the couch in the living room. "I just got a little dizzy."

"Which is why I'm checking you out," Turk told her with a slight grin as he pulled his stethoscope out and listened to her heart. His smile, however, quickly faded as he took her blood pressure and pulse. "Your blood pressure's through the roof," he said, frowning in concern. "Considering the circumstances, that's understandable, but I don't want you taking any chances. You need to lie down until it comes down."

"But...the bakery! I just can't let it burn!"

"The firefighters have it under control," he assured her. "And there's nothing you can really do except worry yourself to death. Is that what you want?"

Put on the spot, she frowned, miffed. "Well, no, of course not."

"Good!" Satisfied, he added, "Now that we've got that settled, I'll stay with you while Rachel checks on the fire. As soon as your blood pressure is in a safer range, we'll talk about going outside again."

She wasn't happy about it, but apparently she knew a stubborn man when she saw one. "All right," she sighed. "Rachel—"

"Oh, no," Rachel said quickly. "I'm not leaving you."

"Sweetheart, I'll be fine."

"You're pale as a ghost and you passed out on the curb. I'm not going anywhere until there's some color in your cheeks and your blood pressure is normal."

"Then I'll go," Turk volunteered smoothly, rising to his feet. "Then I can set both your minds at ease. I won't be gone long. Here's my pager number, Rachel. If you need me, I can be back in twenty seconds."

Even as he hurried out, Rachel wanted to call him back. There was a part of her that didn't want to know if the fire had gutted the bakery, and she could see that same fear in her grandmother's eyes. The bakery had always been there, a part of her grandmother's life, then hers. They both knew every scratch in the old wood floor, every knick in the old countertops in the kitchen. It was impossible to know how many doughnuts and Danish, not to mention cakes and pies and loaves of breads, they'd both made over the years...or the cups of coffee they'd poured for their customers. Everyone in town had had breakfast there at one time or another. It couldn't be gone.

Reading her thoughts, her grandmother broke the silence that had settled over them. "There's plenty of insurance, sweetheart. We haven't lost it."

"I know, Gran," she said huskily, squeezing her hand. "I'm still in shock. I don't know how this happened. I just had the wiring checked last month. And I never walk out the door in the afternoon without checking to make sure all the ovens are off."

"I'm sure it's nothing you did, sweetheart. For all we know, it could have been a short in a refrigerator or a mixer. The fire department will discover where it started. We just have to be patient."

It was hard, however, to sit there and wait. Where was Turk? Rachel wondered, frustrated as fifteen minutes came and went and he still wasn't back. Surely the fire was out by now. If he didn't come back soon, she was paging him.

In the end, she didn't need to. Three minutes later, he strode into the house and announced, "It's out. The fire marshal's still inspecting the building, but it looks like some old rags in the attic were the problem."

Chapter 10

"What do you mean...the fire was deliberately set?" Rachel asked Tom Walker, the fire marshal, thirty minutes later when he came looking for her and her grandmother. "Turk said it started with some rags in the attic."

"It did," he said grimly.

"Then how was it arson?" Evelyn asked, frowning. "The building's over a hundred years old. Those rags must have been up there for years."

"Maybe," he agreed. "Maybe not. The outside stairs lead right to the attic. Anyone could have slipped up there and set the place on fire. The access door to the attic wasn't locked."

"What?" Rachel exclaimed. "Of course it was! We always keep it padlocked."

His gray brows knit in a scowl. "There was no lock on the door. Are you sure you locked it the last time you went up there?"

"I'm positive. I had the heating system checked out three weeks ago and locked the door myself afterward. I haven't been up there since."

"What about Sissy or one of the other employees? Is there a possibility one of them needed the attic for something?"

"Not without me knowing about it," she replied. "I'm the only one with a key, and I keep it on my key chain."

"And it's still there?"

"Well, yes," she began, only to frown as she patted the pocket of her robe for her keys. "There's no reason why it shouldn't be—"

But when she pulled her keys out of her pocket, she saw in an instant that the padlock key was gone. Stunned, she just stared at the spot where it should have been. "I don't understand. I always keep the keys with me. How could one be missing without me being aware of it?"

"Obviously, you must have set them down somewhere," Turk said quietly. "What do you do with them when you go home at the end of the day? Throw them down on a table in your entry hall? Hang them on a hook? What?"

"I drop them in the bottom of my purse," she admitted. "So what are you saying? Someone came in my house, dug in my purse for my keys and stole the one to the padlock? While I was right there in the house?"

"I know it sounds crazy," he replied. "But what other explanation is there?"

"Let's forget the key and look at this from another direction," Tom said. "Who do you know that would set the bakery on fire?"

"No one! This is Hunter's Ridge, for heaven's sake! People don't do that kind of thing here."

"People do that kind of thing everywhere," he replied curtly. "Someone obviously wanted to cause trouble tonight. If they'd really wanted to burn the bakery down, they could have done so. This was just a scare tactic. Have you ticked someone off recently? A boyfriend? An ex-boyfriend? A wannabe boyfriend you didn't look twice at? Maybe even an unhappy customer?"

She couldn't for the life of her think of anyone. Then she remembered Mildred Johnson...and Benny.

"You've remembered something," Turk said, watching her closely.

She hesitated. "Mildred Johnson and her nephew, Benny," she finally admitted. "They were both insulted when I made it clear I wasn't interested in dating Benny, but I can't believe either one of them would set the bakery on fire."

"Why not?"

"Mildred's known Gran forever. And Benny lets his aunt speak for him. To be perfectly honest, I don't think he's got the guts to kill a fly, let alone steal my keys and start a fire in the bakery attic."

Frowning, Tom jotted down both names in his notebook. "I'll question them. Can you think of anyone else who might hold a grudge against you?"

"We had a fight earlier this evening," Turk admitted. "I went home around eleven-thirty and went to bed."

"Alone?"

He nodded grimly. "The sirens woke me up around three. When I realized how close they were, I grabbed my medical bag and ran out the door."

"He didn't do this, Tom," Rachel said huskily. "And neither did Mildred and Benny. It was probably just some teenagers pulling a prank."

"Then how did they get the key to the padlock?"

She didn't have an answer to that, and they all knew it. "I don't know. I suppose someone could have slipped in the back door of the bakery when everyone was occupied at the counter, though you would think someone would have noticed. Oh, and I had new tires put on my car at Pete's Tire Shop on Monday. I didn't bother to leave just the car key— Pete and Gran have been friends all their lives. One of Pete's workers could have slipped the padlock key off, but all of those guys have been with him for years. I just can't see any of them doing that."

"I'll check it out," he promised. "In the meantime, I want you to replace the attic door with a steel door with a dead bolt."

"I'll give Joe Schmidt a call later this morning and see if he can do it today."

"How much damage is there?" Evelyn asked. "Are we going to need to completely remodel it?"

"Thanks to your quick phone call, the damage isn't nearly as bad as it could have been," he replied. "Most of the fire was contained in the attic, but there is some smoke damage downstairs. And water damage, of course," he added. "Everything's pretty waterlogged."

"It could have been worse," Rachel said. "It could have burned to the ground."

"You were lucky," Tom said. "If you think of anyone else who may have done this, give me a call."

Quietly wishing them good-night, he walked out, leaving behind a silence that no one seemed inclined to break. Evelyn finally sighed. "We're not getting anything done sitting around here staring at the walls. We need to get over to the bakery and get to work."

"Oh, no you don't," Turk said quickly, stepping over to the couch and blocking her path before she could even think about rising to her feet. "There'll be no work for you tonight. The only exercise you're going to get is walking to your bed. C'mon. I'll help you."

Far from impressed with his bedside manner, she lifted a delicately arched brow at Rachel. "Are you going to let him talk to me like that?"

Her lips twitched. "I do believe I am. I don't want anything to happen to you, either."

"Nothing's going to happen to me. I'm just going to mop up some water."

"We'll see how you're feeling in the morning and talk about it then," Rachel promised her. "For now, I'd feel better if you went back to bed and tried to get to sleep."

"While you clean up the bakery all by yourself? I don't think so!"

"She's not doing it all by herself," Turk promised her. "I'm going to help her."

Startled, Rachel wanted to jump at his offer, but now that the emergency was over, she couldn't impose on him any more than she already had. Not after he'd made it clear earlier in the evening that he wanted nothing more to do with her. "You don't have to do that," she said quickly. "I appreciate the offer, but this is my problem. I can handle it."

"I want to help."

"No."

Glancing back between the two of them, Evelyn said, "Yes! Or I'll help you."

"No—"

"No, you won't."

Delighted when they both turned on her at once, Evelyn grinned. "Good. Then we're all in agreement. Now that that's settled, I'm going to bed. Keep your phone on, Rachel. I'll call if I need anything." And without another word, she sailed down the hall to her bedroom.

Frustrated, Rachel wasn't the least bit amused when Turk grinned at her. "If you're trying to impress Gran, you can save it. She's gone to bed, remember? She'll never know if you go home or not."

"That's okay," he said easily as he fell into step beside her when she headed home to change into work clothes before going to the bakery. "I'll just stick around, anyway. Just in case you need my help."

Miffed, she didn't understand why he was doing this. He was the one who'd told her to have a nice life! But they reached her house then, and there was no time to demand an explanation. While she was changing, he went to his own house and returned a short time later in paint-splattered jeans and a battered gray sweatshirt he'd cut the sleeves out of. Seconds later, they turned the corner onto Main Street and she forgot all about her irritation with him. A dozen or more people were waiting for her on the bakery's front porch, including Lawrence and Harvey and all of her employees, as well as some of her favorite customers.

Stunned, she stopped in her tracks. "What are you guys doing here?"

"We heard about the fire," Stu Butler said. "We thought we'd help you clean up."

"Yeah," Mick added. "You can't do this all by yourself. Jenny called me, and I called Sissy, and we started calling people. Everybody brought their mops and buckets, and we've got more people coming. Let's get started."

Touched, Rachel didn't know if she wanted to laugh or cry. "You guys are sweethearts. I don't know how to thank you."

"Give us free doughnuts for a month when the bakery's up and running again," Lawrence called out from the back of the crowd.

"You got it," she promised when everyone laughed.

"All right! Then let's get started. We've got a lot of work to do!"

That was an understatement if there ever was one. There was standing water everywhere, not to mention an attic that was full of soggy insulation. Armed with mops and buckets, shovels, face masks and plastic trash bags, all supplied by Stu, who'd opened his hardware store to get what they needed, everyone went to work.

Three hours later, Rachel couldn't believe what her friends and customers had managed to accomplish. All the wet insulation in the attic had been bagged and carted outside, the bakery kitchen and dining room had been mopped dry, and fans had been set up in the attic and downstairs to blow the walls and ceiling dry. The smell of smoke was still strong in the air, and extensive repairs still had to be done before the bakery could open for business again, but overall, Rachel was pleased with the progress that had been made.

"You don't know how much I appreciate this," she told her friends as she gave them each a hug. "It would have taken me days to do all this. Thank you so much."

"No problem," Lawrence said with a grin. "It's the doughnuts, sweetie. Most of us haven't missed breakfast at the bakery in years. We're all going through withdrawal and we haven't even got through the first morning yet."

"I've already thought that out," she chuckled. "Starting tomorrow, I'm going to run the bakery out of my house. So if you can just get through today…"

The words were hardly out of her mouth when a huge cheer went up from the crowd, and she found herself being hugged all over again. Laughing, she returned the hugs and promised to see everyone in the morning. Then she turned around, and everyone had left…everyone, that is, except Turk.

Sitting at one of the chrome tables in the bakery dining area, his long legs stretched out before him and his arms crossed across his chest, he looked as if he was prepared to wait for her forever if he had to. Her eyes met his, and just that quickly, her heart was pounding. "I thought you'd left," she said huskily.

"Not until you do," he replied quietly. "You looked so tired, I was afraid you might not be able to find your way home."

Until then, she hadn't noticed that it took all her energy just to remain upright. "I guess I am a little tired," she admitted. "I didn't get much sleep last night."

His expression turned somber, and just that quickly, she knew he was thinking about last night. And as much as she wanted to forget it, to pretend that it had never happened, she knew she couldn't. It was right there between them every time their eyes met, and she hated it. If he'd just let her explain.

"Would you like to come back to the house for some coffee?" she asked impulsively. "I could make breakfast."

"You don't have to do that."

"I know. I want to. I don't know what I would have done without you this morning."

"You had a lot of help," he pointed out. "I didn't do any more than anyone else."

"Yes, you did," she insisted huskily. "You have every right to hate my guts and you still helped. Why? You could have walked away. I certainly wouldn't have blamed you if you had. No one would have."

"You needed help," he said simply. "Nothing else mattered."

He would have said the same thing to a stranger,

and that hurt. "If you could set aside your anger for that, can you set it aside long enough to listen to me?" she asked quietly. "There's something I need to tell you. Maybe then you'll understand why I did what I did."

He should have said no. He wasn't interested in listening to excuses. He knew who she was now and there was nothing to talk about. But her eyes were dark with a pain he couldn't ignore, and dammit, he wanted a reason to forgive her. Before the fire last night, he'd dreamed of her, rolled over and reached for the phone in his sleep before he even realized what he was doing. He was in trouble. Big trouble. She'd somehow gotten to him, and he cared about her more than he wanted to. There was no way he could make himself walk away from her.

Later, he knew that was going to bother him, but for now, all he could say was, "Coffee sounds good. Let's go."

For a moment, he thought she was going to cry. Sudden tears glistened in her eyes, but she quickly blinked them away. "Let me lock up, then we can go."

Ten minutes later, she joined him at her kitchen table and served them both steaming cups of coffee and thick slices of banana nut bread. Turk would have sworn he wasn't hungry, but the second he took a bite of the bread and it melted in his mouth, he realized he was starving. "This is fantastic!"

She smiled. "It's Gran's recipe. She won first place at the state fair with it."

"I can believe it. What's wrong with the men in Hunter's Ridge? Your grandfather died years ago, didn't he? Evelyn's a damn fine-looking woman. Why didn't some man snatch her up years ago?"

"Oh, they tried," she chuckled. "But the only man she's ever loved died thirty years ago. She hasn't given anyone a second glance since."

"Your grandfather was lucky to have a woman love him that much."

She smiled at the memory of her grandfather. "He wasn't the only one who was lucky. He adored Gran and didn't care who knew it. They had a wonderful relationship."

Watching her, Turk felt an emotion he couldn't put a name to tug at his heart. She looked so sad and wistful, and it didn't take a genius to figure out that she'd never come close to having the kind of relationship her grandparents had had. Did she think she never would? Was that why she'd decided to get pregnant by a stranger? She'd given up any hope of finding happiness with a man and just wanted a baby to help cut the heartache of loneliness?

Torn between irritation and confusion, he wanted to hit her with a dozen questions, but in the end, he only asked one. "What is it you wanted to tell me?"

She hesitated, only to abruptly come to her feet and walk over to the coffee pot to refill their mugs.

She didn't, however, return to the table, but stood instead with her back to the table as she cupped her mug in both hands and stared unseeingly out the window over the sink.

"I got married my senior year of college," she said huskily. "I was young and silly and in love. The only thing we needed for everything to be perfect was a baby."

His jaw tightened. "You already told me—"

"I didn't tell you this," she said quietly, and turned to face him. Turk had never seen such stark pain on a woman's face in his life. "I tried to get pregnant the first year we were married...and the next...and the year after that. I never could."

"Why? You did go to the doctor, didn't you? What did he say the problem was?"

"He couldn't find anything."

"Then your husband was the one with the problem."

"The doctor said the same thing, but Jason refused to be tested. He didn't want to be blamed for *my* infertility."

"But you weren't infertile—that's the whole point! What a jerk. It's not that difficult to be tested. If he wanted a baby—"

"But he didn't," she cut in. "I did. He really wanted nothing to do with fatherhood or babies. That's why he had a vasectomy before we were married without telling me."

"What?"

"Seven years after we got married, he finally confessed," she said flatly, hugging herself. "I wanted to try in-vitro, and he refused to even consider it. We had a big fight, and when I accused him of not wanting a baby, he finally admitted it. I filed for divorce three days later."

Stunned, Turk couldn't begin to imagine what she must have felt. She'd tried to get pregnant for seven *years,* and all the while, the jackass she'd been married to had known she was wasting her time. And he'd never said a word.

Furious for her, he could only imagine what she'd felt when she discovered the truth. "You must have been devastated," he said huskily.

"I've never felt so betrayed in my life," she said simply. "I wasted seven years of my life on a liar. Do you know how stupid I felt? I tried everything to get pregnant. And every time I failed, he blamed me. I had to be the one with the problem—there was nothing wrong with him. My hormones were off…I needed estrogen…I had some kind of female problem…I was sterile. He had one excuse after another for *my* infertility. And like a fool, I believed him. It had to be me. So I went to one specialist after another, had test after test after test, and the doctors could find nothing."

When tears pooled in her eyes, he almost reached for her then and there. She'd been through hell, and the one person in the world she should have been able to trust the most had turned out to be the last man on earth she should have believed. No wonder she'd decided to have a baby by herself. She'd probably never trust another man in her life, and he couldn't say he blamed her.

"Why didn't you tell me this before now?" he asked gruffly. "It explains a hell of a lot."

"It's not something I generally talk about," she admitted with a grimace. "No one likes admitting they've been taken in by a liar. Especially when they were married to the jackass for seven years."

"The only thing you had on your mind was getting pregnant," he pointed out. "How could you have guessed that the jerk had had a vasectomy? It's not like it was tattooed on his forehead or anything. And he was your husband. If he'd never given you any reason to doubt him in the past, why wouldn't you believe him?"

"I was married to him," she said with a shrug. "I should have known what kind of man he was." Her eyes meeting his, she added, "And that doesn't excuse my own behavior. I don't know what I was thinking. I just wanted a baby so bad I was desperate."

"You have plenty of time, Rachel."

"Technically...maybe. But I can hear the clock ticking, which is why I came up with the crazy idea of just getting pregnant by the first decent man I could find, then walking away. It was a stupid plan—I know that now. And just for the record, you were never part of that plan. And I'm sorry I didn't tell you the truth. And even after I met you, I never tried to trick you."

He couldn't deny that—he hadn't forgotten that she'd insisted he use a condom. "So…this plan of yours…are you through with it? Because if you're still looking for a sperm donor, we have nothing more to say to each other."

"No more crazy plans," she assured him thickly. "I promise."

When tears spilled over her lashes and she quickly wiped them away, he wanted to reach for her, to pull her into his arms and assure her that everything was going to be all right. But he couldn't. Not yet. She'd destroyed his trust in her, and it would take time to get that back. In the meantime, he intended to move very, very slowly. She already had his heart tied up with string—she just didn't know it. And he intended to keep it that way for as long as possible.

"Now that we've got that settled, why don't you go to bed?" he told her. "It was a long night. You've got to be exhausted."

If circumstances had been different, she would have asked him to stay just because it *had* been a long night, and she didn't want to be alone. She ached to feel his arms around her, but it wasn't going to happen. She only had to look at his face to know that.

Her heart breaking, she forced a weak smile. "I am tired. I'll probably be out the second my head hits the pillow." Suddenly remembering that he should be at his clinic, working, she gasped, "Oh, my God! I completely forgot you're supposed to be at the clinic! You shouldn't have stayed and helped with the cleanup—you had work to do!"

"It's okay," he assured her. "I called and canceled my morning appointments. I'll catch a quick nap and go in after lunch."

When she walked him to the door, she knew she should have thanked him again, then let him go. But the ache inside her was too deep. Giving in to it, knowing he was going to stiffen the second she touched him but unable to stop herself, she stepped forward to give him a quick hug. "I'll see you later," she said huskily. "Thanks again, for all your help."

He didn't return her hug, but then again, he didn't push her away, either. "Get some sleep," he replied. "I'll check in on you later and make sure you're doing all right."

Standing at her front door, she watched him cut across her yard to his and waited him for him to turn and wave. He never did. Before she even shut the door, tears were streaming down her face. Hurt, exhausted, emotionally spent, she made her way to her bedroom and crawled into bed, clothes and all. With a sob, she buried her head in her pillow and gave in to the heartache ripping her apart from the inside out. Her pillow soon damp with tears, she cried and cried and never knew when she fell asleep.

Hidden in the overgrown bushes that flanked the house across the street, Laureen watched Turk cross the yard to his own house and disappear inside. Bastard. She'd seen the hug Betty Crocker had given him, and she hadn't been fooled by the fact that he hadn't hugged the little witch back. The chemistry between them was almost palpable. Damn them, they'd made love!

Enraged, she wanted to kill them both. How dare they! Did they think she wouldn't find out? That they could keep their relationship a secret from her? She wasn't an idiot. He hadn't let the bitch out of his sight from the moment he'd come running at the first sound of the fire truck's siren. He was cheating on her, and by God, this was going to stop! Turk was hers. The second she'd met him in Dallas, she'd known he was the man she'd been waiting all her life for. And no one, especially a little skinny-assed hussy in a baker's apron, was going to steal him away from her.

Infuriated, she couldn't remember the last time she'd been so angry. If Betty Crocker thought she had problems before, just wait. Laureen was going to make her wish she'd never laid eyes on her man, let alone touched him.

Chapter 11

The afternoon should have flown by. When he arrived at the clinic after lunch, he hardly had time to deal with one medical crisis before another one walked in the door. The pace was frantic, the waiting room full. He didn't even take an afternoon break, and still, the afternoon seemed to drag by.

Because all he wanted to do was call Rachel.

He didn't, but it wasn't easy. Over the course of the afternoon, he lost track of the number of times he picked up the phone, only to hang up when he realized what he was doing. He couldn't stop thinking about the pain in her eyes when

she'd told him what her ex had done to her. That
kind of betrayal might have broken another
woman. How had she stood it? She was so strong.
Even last night, when the business she loved was
burning, she'd found a way to smile afterward
when her customers had showed up to help her
clean the place up. And he admired the hell out of
her for that.

And it was that kind of thinking that was going
to get him in trouble.

Frowning, he was quickly scribbling notes for his
medical transcriber when his cell phone rang.
Normally, he wouldn't have taken it, but when he
checked the number displayed on the screen, he
lifted a brow in surprise. Why was his mother
calling? She never called when he was working.

"Mom? What's wrong?"

"What's wrong?" she demanded. "I was about
to ask you the same question! I can't believe you
got married without telling me or your father! Do
you know how hurt we are? I know we didn't
support your move to Hunter's Ridge, but that
didn't mean you had to cut us out of your life! What
were you thinking?"

Surprised, he laughed. "Is this a joke?"

"Do I sound like I'm joking?" his mother
snapped. "Where did you find this woman? She has
absolutely no class whatsoever!"

"What woman? Mom, honest to God, I don't

know what you're talking about. Who have you been talking to?"

"That's what I've been trying to tell you! Your wife!"

Confused, aware of the curious looks he was drawing from his staff, he stepped into his office and quickly shut the door so he could continue the conversation in private. "Okay," he growled, "let's start this conversation over. I don't have a wife— I'm not married and I certainly wouldn't get married without telling my parents. So who have you been talking to? And don't tell me my wife," he said quickly. "I don't have a wife or a fiancée or anything else."

"Then you'd better listen to your answering machine," his mother retorted. "Because there's a message from your *wife* on there that I'm sure you'd be interested in."

Scowling, he snapped, "I'll call you right back."

Hanging up, he quickly punched in his home number and waited impatiently for the answering machine to click on. He didn't have to wait long. "Hi, this is Laureen Garrison, Turk's new wife. We'd love to come to the phone right now, but we can't. You know how it is with newlyweds. We're too busy making love. Leave a message at the beep and we'll call you back when we come up for air."

For a second, all Turk heard was the roar of his blood in his ears. "Dammit to hell!" Furious, he slammed down the phone, cussing a blue streak. How dare she! How the hell had she got into his house? When he got his hands on her, she was going to wish she'd never been born!

"Dr. Garrison, there's a—" Tapping on his office door, his nurse stuck her head in the door, only to blink at the fury on his face. "I'm sorry. I didn't mean to intrude. Mrs. James is in examining room number 2. She sliced her finger on a can—"

"Check to see when she last had a tetanus shot, and I'll be right there." Glancing at his watch, he frowned. "I'm going to take a half hour break after I see Mrs. James. I've got some business I've got to take care of at home."

"Yes, sir," she assured him. "Of course."

Still seething, Turk hurriedly stitched up Becky James's finger, then rushed home to see what damage Laureen had done to his house. He didn't think for one second that she'd broken in just to change the greeting on his answering machine. She'd probably trashed the place and taken whatever struck her fancy just because she could. Just thinking about her going through his things infuriated him. This time, she'd gone too far. By God, he was calling the cops and they could take care of her. He was sick of dealing with her.

The front door to his house was locked, but he didn't unlock it and go inside. Instead, he reached for his cell phone and called the police. When a patrol car pulled up in front of his house ten minutes later, he sighed in relief at the sight of the officer who stepped from the car. It was Doug Walker— and he already knew all about Laureen.

"Hey, Dr. Garrison," the younger man greeted him with an outstretched hand. "It sounds like you're having problems again."

"I'm afraid so," he said grimly. "I got a call from my mother this afternoon. Apparently, Laureen found a way to change the outgoing message on my answering machine. I don't know how she could have done it without breaking in."

"Have you been inside yet?"

"No," he said curtly. "I was afraid she trashed the place, so I thought it would be better to let you go in first."

"Smart move. Have you heard from her since she showed up at the clinic that day?" he asked as he examined the front door to see if the lock had been forced. "What about a key? Is there any way she could have gotten one without you knowing it?"

"No!" Just the thought of Laureen having a key to his house turned his blood cold. He'd already changed the locks once—he was changing them again, first thing in the morning. "I don't know if she's got a key or not—she certainly wouldn't let that stop her from getting in if she was determined to break in." Swearing, he added, "I should have known she was too quiet. Now she's changed the message on my answering machine and told everyone we got married. You can just imagine how that went over with my parents."

Doug whistled softly. "My mother would have had a stroke."

"Mine nearly did. You've got to do something about this, man. She's getting more daring."

"Let's see what she's done," he said grimly, and waited for Turk to unlock the front door, then preceded him inside.

"My office is through there," Turk told him, nodding to the first door on the left. "The answering machine's on the desk."

Easily finding it, Doug pulled on gloves and hit the play message button on the answering machine. Immediately, Laureen's too bright, too smug voice filled the office. "Hi, this is Laureen Garrison, Turk's new wife. We'd love to come to the phone right now—"

"Well, she's got nerve, I'll give her that," Doug said as the message played out and Turk swore roundly. "She's pretty damn stupid, though. She might as well have signed a confession—she didn't even try to disguise her identity."

"She's too arrogant for that," Turk retorted. "She doesn't think I'll press charges—or even if I do, that she'll be caught."

"Then she's in for a rude awakening, isn't she.

Let's check the rest of the house. If she's as brash as she seems, there's a good chance that the message on the answering machine isn't the only surprise she's left for you."

Turk didn't doubt that, but as he followed the detective through the house, he was stunned to discover how sick Laureen really was. She'd tucked several sexy nightgowns, not to mention five pairs of lacy panties, in the top drawer of his dresser. And on his pillow, she'd left a picture of herself that looked like it belonged in a porn magazine.

Swearing, he wanted to burn the damn thing, but Doug slipped it into a plastic evidence bag before he could even reach for it, let alone destroy it. "What do you really know about this woman's background, Dr. Garrison?"

"I didn't run a background check on her, detective, if that's what you're asking."

"Maybe you should have," he retorted. "So you don't know if she's done this kind of thing in the past?"

"I would think she must have. She's a damn stalker! Surely I'm not her first victim."

"Unfortunately, this kind of thing isn't always reported," he said grimly. "Did she ever mention any other hospitals where she worked?"

He started to say no, only to remember a conversation they'd had the first time he met her. "Not a hospital, no, but when I made a comment about her Southern accent, she said she was originally from New Orleans. You might check all the hospitals in the area."

He made a note. "Now, what about your parents? Does she know where they live?"

Surprised, he frowned. "Not that I know of. Why?"

"She's a stalker, Dr. Garrison. "She's not logical. If she thinks your family or anyone you're close to is going to take you away from her, they could be in a great deal of danger. You need to warn your parents. What about a girlfriend? You were at the fire at the bakery early this morning, weren't you? With Rachel Martin? Is there a possibility this Laureen woman could have seen the two of you together?"

Turk swore. He hadn't even thought of that. "She's a night owl," he said. "She could have very easily been out there in the shadows, watching our every move."

"Then you need to warn Rachel—"

"Warn Rachel about what?" she asked from the doorway. When both men whirled to face her, she said, "I saw the patrol car. I was afraid something else was wrong. So what do I need to be warned about?"

Biting back a curse, Turk hesitated. After the fire and everything she'd been through last night, the last thing he wanted to do was lay another worry on her. But Doug Walker was right. She had a right to know that there was a crazy woman out there who could, at any moment, decide to make her life miserable just because she'd made the mistake of having a relationship with him.

"I'm being stalked," he said flatly.

"What? By whom?"

"Her name's Laureen Becker. I took her out a couple of times in Dallas, then broke things off before I moved here. Apparently, she somehow found out where I was and is now trying to force her way into my life. She showed up at the clinic last week with a serious burn on her arm. There was no question that she'd deliberately burned herself."

"Oh, my God!"

His face carved in harsh lines, he grimaced. "I told her she needed some professional help, and she flipped out. I'd never seen her so enraged. Maybe that's why she broke in today, to get back at me."

"Here?" she said, surprised. "She broke in here? How do you know it was her?"

"Because she changed the greeting on my answering machine and told whoever cared to call that she was my wife," he replied curtly.

"That wasn't very bright of her, but I still don't see what any of this has to do with me. I don't even know the woman."

"There's a good chance that she probably saw me leave your house after the fire. That would explain her breaking in here suddenly, with no warning. She would be livid if she saw me with another woman."

Rachel paled at his words. "How livid? Is there

a possibility that she's been watching you for a while? That she might have seen the two of us together earlier in the week? Maybe she's the one who set the bakery on fire."

Turk had been so disgusted with the message that Laureen had left on his answering machine that he hadn't even made the connection that she might have already gone after Rachel out of spite. Suddenly, her prankish break-in at his house became a hell of a lot more serious. If she could get in his house so easily, she would have no trouble breaking into Rachel's. Just thinking about what Laureen might do to her when she was home alone, possibly asleep and unaware of the danger she was in, scared the hell out of him.

"You're right," he retorted. "I don't know what I was thinking. Of course she would do it."

Stepping over to the phone, he quickly called the clinic. When his office manager answered, he sighed in relief. "Janice! Thank God! I need you to check some information on a patient for me. Get on the computer and get me the home address for Laureen Becker. You remember—she was in last week for a burn—"

"Trust me, I haven't forgotten her name," she said dryly. "She's the one that burned herself just to get your attention. There are a lot of sick people in the world, Dr. Garrison. Don't take this wrong, but you need to steer clear of that one. She's a fruit loop."

"You won't get an argument out of me," he retorted. "What's her address?"

"It's 415 Dawson Creek," she said promptly. "Apartment 302."

"Thanks," he growled, quickly jotting it down. "I owe you one." Hanging up, he handed Doug Laureen's address. "This is where she claimed she was living last week. I wouldn't be surprised if it's a phony address, but it's all we've got to go on."

"What about her phone number?" he asked.

"She only called a few times, and she blocked the number every time," he replied. "I don't know if she was on her cell, a land line, or a pay phone halfway across the country."

"Where did you meet this woman?" Rachel asked, frowning. "She sounds crazy."

"She was a nurse at St. Joseph's Children's Hospital in Plano," he replied. "She seemed nice…at first. Then I went out with her a second time and discovered she was already planning our wedding. She'd even bought a dress!"

"Are you serious?" Rachel gasped. "How long had you known her?"

"Six days," he retorted. "That's when I realized that she was too far out there for me. I was already planning to move to Hunter's Ridge, but I didn't tell her that. And I know none of my friends did. I still don't know how she found me."

"Trust me, we'll do everything we can to find

out," Doug promised. "In the meantime, if you have any more problems with Ms. Becker or remember anything else about her, give me a call. I keep my cell phone on all the time, so don't hesitate to call."

Taking the business card that he held out to him, Turk said flatly, "I'm more worried about her showing up here again or at Rachel's. She's a loose cannon. You never know what she's going to do."

"Just don't do anything stupid—like take the law into your own hands," he warned. "Then you'll end up in jail, too, and trust me, she's not worth it."

"So now we just have to sit and wait and worry?" Rachel asked. "Is that what you're saying?"

"Unfortunately, yes. Change your locks. The lady's already proved she's damn clever. In her mind, Dr. Garrison is hers. If she thinks she's losing him—or worse yet, that he was never really hers to begin with—watch out. That's when she's really going to become dangerous. Whatever you do, don't underestimate her."

Long after he left, his words hung in the air between Rachel and Turk. Finally, he was the one who broke the silence. "I don't like the idea of you being alone," he said gruffly. "Laureen's a nutcase. I wouldn't put anything past her."

"I'll be careful," she assured him. "And I really won't be alone—at least not for a few hours, anyway. The insurance adjuster's meeting me at the bakery, then I'm going to call some of my customers who are in construction and see about getting some bids. I don't even want to think about how long it's going to take to make all the repairs. I'm going to be running the business out of my kitchen for months!"

He should have been relieved. She was safe—for the moment—and he didn't have to worry about her. But his jaw clenched on an oath just at the thought of Laureen somehow getting to her, hurting her. "Just call me every hour and let me know you're all right. Okay?"

"I'll be fine—"

"Just humor me and call me every hour, will you?" he insisted. "Otherwise, I'm going to be running over to the bakery every chance I get just to make sure you're all right. Of course, if you want me running over there…"

Her lips twitched. "I'll call. Okay? Satisfied?"

If circumstances had been different, he would have laughed at that. *Satisfied?* He hadn't realized just how dissatisfied he was until right that minute. She was in danger, dammit! Because of him. Did she know what that did to him? He didn't want to let her out of his sight, out of his arms. Satisfied? Hell, no, he wasn't satisfied.

"Just be careful," he growled, and surprised them both when he reached for her.

Rachel hadn't realized how much she needed him to hold her, kiss her, until she was in his arms and his mouth was on hers. Tears stinging her eyes, she wanted to ask him if he had forgiven her for her crazy plans to get pregnant, but surely he wouldn't kiss her as if he were starving for the taste of her if he was still angry with her. Surely he wouldn't wrap her tight against him when she kissed him back unless he wanted her as much as she wanted him. Because if he didn't, she was going to be devastated.

Fighting tears, she told herself to keep it light when he finally released her. It wasn't easy. The teasing smile that curved her mouth when her eyes met his cost her dearly. "Wow. What was that for?"

"Just because," he rasped. "A man shouldn't have to have a reason for kissing a pretty woman. C'mon. I'll walk you to the bakery."

His clinic was in the opposite direction—she should have thanked him for the offer and all his help and sent him on his way. But how could she deny herself another ten minutes of his time? Her heart pounding like a schoolgirl's, she fell into step beside him.

After he left her at the bakery, however, she had little time to think about him. The insurance adjuster arrived at the bakery five minutes after she did and went through the building with her. Just seeing the damage again made Rachel sick at heart. If her grandmother hadn't smelled the smoke, the place would have burned to the ground. Fortunately, there was no serious structural damage, and the check the adjuster presented her with was more than adequate to cover the repairs. He'd hardly wished her good luck and walked out the door before she was on the phone, calling customers who could help her put the bakery back together.

Once the word was out, electricians, plumbers, contractors and dry wall hangers were descending on her and the bakery, ready to offer assistance. She didn't, however, forget to call Turk.

"Hello, Dr. Garrison," she said in a teasingly businesslike voice when he answered his cell phone. "This is Rachel Martin calling to report in, as directed. Everything's fine, Doctor. There's been no sign of the evil one. I'm perfectly safe. Will there be anything else, Doctor?"

"Clod," he chuckled. "I'm just trying to keep you safe, and all I get is criticism. You would think a woman would appreciate it, but *noooo!* You want to give me a hard time."

"Wah! What a baby."

"See? What'd I tell you? There you go again."

She hadn't realized how desperately she needed him to tease her again until then. Blinking back tears, she asked huskily, "Did I say thank you?"

"Yes, you did. You're welcome. You don't have to keep telling me, you know. I'd do just about anything for one of your doughnuts."

Groaning, she laughed. "I should have known. It always comes down to the doughnuts. Just for the record, I start serving at six in the morning at my house. And tomorrow morning, everything's free."

"What? I thought you were going to do that when the bakery reopened."

"I was," she said wryly. "But the repairs could take a while, so I decided to do it tomorrow. I've got to haul all my equipment over to the house, but I'm going to need it, anyway."

"I'll help you move everything if you can wait until after the clinic closes," he told her. "I've got patients all afternoon."

"Oh, that's okay—I'll have it done by then. I'd like to have everything set up as soon as possible so I'm not up half the night getting the kitchen in order. If you get off early, though…"

"You'll be the first to know it," he promised. "Just call me, okay? And let me know you're okay?"

"I'm fine," she assured him. "And the police are keeping a close watch on me, Turk. The whole town is crawling with cops. This Laureen woman would have to be an idiot to show her face in Hunter's Ridge when everyone and their brother is looking for her."

"I know that and you know it," he agreed, "but she's crazy. Don't underestimate her. Remember, she tracked me to Hunter's Ridge and found a way to get into my house and change my answering machine. My God, she even burned herself so she could get into the clinic to see me. There's no way to predict what she'll do next."

A cold shiver slid down her spine. "I'll be careful," she said huskily. "I promise."

Thankful that Christopher Dunkin and his partner, Jeff Valdez, were parked in their police car at the curb in front of the bakery, she started boxing up everything she would need in the morning. Then, with Christopher and Jeff following her home, she got her car, drove back to the bakery, and started loading her car. Forty minutes later, she pulled into her driveway and smiled at the sight of Chris and Jeff, who were parked across the street and were watching her house. She knew all the cops in town—at one time or another during the afternoon, they all stopped by the bakery for coffee and dough-nuts. They would make sure nothing happened to her on their watch.

She would have to tease Turk later for being so paranoid, she told herself as she carried her first load into the house. After last night, Laureen had to know the entire town was on the look out for her. The woman might be crazy, but Rachel sincerely doubted she was stupid. She'd probably headed back to Dallas just seconds after she'd set the rags smoldering in the bakery attic. Hopefully, she'd never show her face in Hunter's Ridge again.

Holding on to that thought, Rachel carried one load after another into the house, then waved to Chris and Jeff as she lifted the last box from her car. They grinned, but made no move to leave. Obviously, they were there for the duration. Relieved, she hurried inside and shut and locked the door with a sigh. She was safe. Now all she had to do was figure out where she was going to put everything she'd brought from the bakery in her small kitchen.

Frowning at the thought as she stepped into the kitchen, she started to set the box of utensils she was carrying onto the island. That was as far as she got. A split second later, someone grabbed her hair. She didn't even have time to scream before she found a knife pressed to her throat.

Chapter 12

The box of cooking utensils Rachel was holding fell to the floor with a loud clatter, but all she heard was the nearly silent whisper of a knife as its cold, hard blade came to rest against her bare throat. Horrified, she froze. "Laureen?"

At her hoarse whisper, the grip on her hair tightened ever so slightly, holding her still while the knife was pressed tighter against her skin. "So you were expecting me," the other woman purred. "How lovely. That makes what I have to do all the easier. I don't have to explain myself."

Needing to swallow, afraid of the razor-sharp edge of the knife against her throat, Rachel fought panic and just barely won. "There seems to be a misunderstanding," she told her desperately. "Turk and I aren't—"

"Liar! I've seen you with him. *I know!*"

"Then you misunderstood. I don't want Turk. I just want a baby! Ask him. He'll tell you. When he found out that I was just looking for a sperm donor, he was livid."

"He touched you," she whispered. "He made love to you. Do you know how that sickens me? He's my husband—not yours. He knows that."

She sounded so convincing that Rachel might have believed her if she hadn't known better. "Laureen, you have to listen—"

"He's my husband! He was meant for me. I knew it the second I laid eyes on him, and so did he. And now he's ruined everything. Because of you! You tempted him. Don't deny it!" she cried when Rachel started to protest.

"You were all over him and he loved every minute of it. And you're both going to pay for that. No one takes what's mine and lives to tell about it."

The threat was soft, little more than a whisper... and a promise. Rachel shivered and felt her fear turn to terror in the blink of an eye. When Turk had warned her Laureen was crazy, she'd taken the announcement with a grain of salt. Turk had rejected Laureen, and Rachel could understand why she would be upset, especially if she didn't want the relationship to end. But this was more than *upset*. This was insanity.

And an unsuspecting Turk was going to walk right into the middle of it when he stopped by to see her after work.

Horrified, she knew she had to do something! But what? Chris and Jeff were parked right outside in their patrol car, watching the house from across the street. All she had to do was scream…and her throat would be slit before she could manage anything more than a muffled cry. She'd bleed to death, right on her kitchen floor, and no one would be the wiser until Turk walked in and Laureen stuck a knife into him, too.

No! This couldn't be happening. There had to be something she could do. There was no question that Laureen was dead serious—she held the knife like a woman who knew how to use it. Terrified, Rachel knew she couldn't let that stop her from doing something. Laureen was going to kill her, anyway. If she couldn't save herself, she had to at least try to save Turk.

Her heart slamming against her ribs, she looked desperately around the kitchen. If she just had some kind of weapon of her own…

Her eyes fell on the box of utensils she'd dropped when Laureen grabbed her. They were scattered across the floor at their feet. If she could just reach them…

Later, she never remembered making a conscious decision to move. One second she was standing rigid with a knife at her throat, and the next, her knees buckled. Caught off guard, Laureen instinctively moved to catch her, and that was all the advantage Rachel needed. Even as she hit the floor, she snatched up a rolling pin and came up swinging. Before Laureen could even guess her intentions, she knocked the knife out of her hand and sent it sliding across the kitchen floor.

"You bitch!" Laureen cried, and sprang for the weapon at the same time Rachel did. When her fingers closed on the knife first, she turned on Rachel with an evil smile. "Now...where were we?"

She should have called by now.

Finishing up the last of his paperwork, Turk glanced at the clock on the wall in his office and frowned. She'd called him at the top of the hour every hour all afternoon, and she'd always been right on time. So where was she?

He reminded himself that she was moving her bakery equipment from the bakery to her house—she'd probably lost track of time, which was perfectly understandable. She was opening for business in the morning at six and had a lot on her mind. The least he could do was cut her some slack and quit worrying. The police were watching every move she made. She was perfectly safe.

So why was he so worried?

Because she had been so diligent about calling precisely at the top of the hour.

Something was wrong. He didn't want to believe it, but the thought gnawed at him, eating him from the inside out. Glancing at the clock again, he knew that he should at least give her a few more minutes, but he couldn't. Reaching for the phone, he quickly punched in her cell phone number.

When she didn't answer by the fourth ring, he knew she was in serious trouble. But how? The police had been watching her all afternoon—they would have followed her home when she left the bakery. Surely, she was perfectly safe. So where the hell was she? And where was Laureen? If she wanted to hurt Rachel, she wouldn't let a cop parked at the curb stop her.

His heart stopping dead in his chest at the thought, he ran for the door. "Call the police and tell them to send backup to Rachel Martin's house," he shouted at his nurse. "Laureen's there."

Running the three blocks to Rachel's house, all he could think about was Laureen...and how determined she was to marry him. He didn't want to think she would hurt Rachel, but he couldn't forget the look in her eye when she'd admitted burning herself just so she could see him. She was sick...crazy. And that scared the hell out of him. If she would hurt herself, she wouldn't hesitate to hurt Rachel.

Coming around the corner at a dead run, he immediately spied the patrol car sitting across the street in front of Rachel's house. The officers inside didn't have a clue anything was wrong. "Laureen's inside," he yelled. "She—"

Suddenly, from inside the house, a woman screamed in terror.

Turk paled. *"Rachel!"*

He never remembered kicking in the door. A split second later, he charged into the house, only to stumble to a stop at the entrance to the kitchen, his blood turning to ice at the sight of Laureen advancing toward Rachel with a butcher knife clutched in her hand. Her eyes were wild and enraged, the glint of insanity there for anyone to see.

"You bitch!" Laureen screamed at Rachel as she took a blind step back, then another, without ever taking her eyes off the knife. "You've ruined everything!"

"Back off, Laureen!" Turk growled. "She didn't do anything. I broke things off with you before I even met her."

"No, you didn't! You just wanted me to chase you. Then she came on the scene and you wouldn't even look at me." Never taking her narrowed gaze from Rachel, she stalked her like a cat with a mouse, slashing the air again and again, retreating only when Rachel swung the rolling pin at her.

Her face totally devoid of color, her heart hammering against her ribs, Rachel didn't dare look anywhere but at the glittering blade of the butcher knife that Laureen cut the air with it. She didn't doubt for a minute that the other woman would slash her to pieces right before Turk's eyes if she miscalculated and swung the rolling pin too late.

"You're not going to get away with this," Rachel told her. "Too many people know you started the fire last night."

"That's right," Turk said. "Look around you, Laureen. There're are cops at every door and window, just waiting to shoot the damn knife out of your hand. If you don't believe me, look behind you."

For a long minute, she didn't look anywhere but at Rachel. Then, lightning quick, she glanced over her shoulder and spied Chris standing right behind Turk in the kitchen doorway with his service revolver drawn and aimed directly at her.

"The house is surrounded, miss," he growled. "Give it up before someone gets hurt."

"No!" she screamed. "Get back! All of you! You can't stop me. I have to do this!" And with no more warning than that, she lunged.

Caught off guard, Rachel jumped back…and lost her balance. She stumbled and dropped the rolling pin. In a heartbeat, Laureen was on her.

Just that quickly, something snapped in Turk. "No!" His bellow of rage rattling the windows, he launched himself at Laureen, snatching her away from Rachel one-handed. "Enough! You hurt her and I swear I'll—"

Cursing him to hell and back, Laureen swung wildly at him...and stabbed him in the side. Lightning quick, she jabbed at him again, making him swear as blood dripped from a second cut on his arm.

"Stop!" Rachel screamed. "You're going to kill him!"

Ignoring her, Laureen aimed straight for his heart. She never even saw Rachel snatch up the rolling pin again. It came crashing down own on her head. Without a sound, she collapsed on the floor.

Christopher rushed forward with his gun drawn, but Laureen never moved. Half the Hunter's Ridge police department seemed to race into the kitchen at that moment, but Rachel hardly noticed. Dropping the rolling pin, she hurried to Turk's side. "Oh, God, you're bleeding! We need an ambulance!"

"I'm fine," he assured her, checking the slashes on his side and arm. "I just need a few stitches. I don't need to go to the hospital for that."

"So...what? You're going to stitch your own knife wounds?"

"No, of course not," he chuckled. "The EMTs can take care of it. It's not complicated."

She wanted to argue, but one look at his set chin had the words dying in her throat. "It's your call," she replied as a fresh-faced EMT stepped forward to examine his cuts.

Laureen stirred then, spitting curses as she pushed herself up off the floor, but she wasn't going anywhere fast. Chris and Jeff stood close guard while an EMT the size of linebacker checked her out. "She's fine," he announced flatly. "She's got a hard head."

"You got that right," Turk retorted. "Get her out of here."

"No!" Laureen screamed, slapping at Chris as he tried to handcuff her. "Don't touch me! The bitch attacked me. I had a right to protect myself."

Distracted by Chris, she didn't notice that Jeff had moved behind her until he suddenly grabbed her hands, snapped them behind her back, and handcuffed her before she could do anything but gasp in outrage. "You have the right to remain silent. Anything you say can and may be used against you…"

"Bastard!" she screamed. "Turk, make them let me go. Tell them you love me. We're engaged!"

"No, we're not," he told her coldly. "We went out twice, Laureen. *Twice!* I didn't even kiss you."

"But you wanted to! I know you did. We can work this out."

"There's nothing to work out. I don't love you. I never loved you and never will. You tried to kill Rachel!"

"She deserved it! She was going to take you away from me!"

"She can't take me away from you. Don't you get it? *I was never yours!*"

"Don't say that! Turk—"

Disgusted, he turned his attention back to the young EMT who was stitching up his cuts. "Are we done yet?"

"Just a few more stitches and you're good to go, sir."

"Let's go," Jeff growled at Laureen. Grabbing her arm, he pushed her toward the front door.

"Turk! Help me! Don't be this way!"

Turk never spared them a glance as Chris and Jeff escorted her outside to the waiting patrol car. A second later, the EMTs packed up their first aid kits, loaded them into the ambulance and advised Turk to keep his wounds clean and dry. Suddenly, everyone was gone.

In the silence left behind, Turk reached for Rachel's hand and drew her with him into the living room. "Sit," he growled softly, urging her down to the couch. "You're as pale as a ghost. Are you all right? When you didn't call, it scared the hell out of me. I knew she had you."

"She was waiting for me when I brought the last load of supplies from the bakery," she said thickly, wrapping her arms around herself as a shiver danced over her skin. "The second I stepped into the kitchen, she grabbed me and held a knife to my throat. I thought she was going to kill me right there on the spot."

"So did I," he rasped, slipping an arm around her

shoulders to draw her against him. "I've never been so afraid for anyone in my life. I didn't think I'd get here in time—"

"Don't," she choked. "When she went after you with the knife, I thought—"

"What?" he asked huskily when she hesitated. "Tell me."

She shouldn't have—he was going to break her heart and telling him would only make it more painful—but he only had to take her hand in his to pull the words from her. "I was afraid I'd lost you," she said softly, lifting her gaze to his. "Not that you were ever mine to lose," she added with a wry grimace. "I know I blew that—"

"Rachel—"

"It's okay," she cut in. "I know what I did—"

"You don't have to do this. If you'd just—"

"Yes, I do. I don't know what I was thinking. I just wanted a baby so badly...."

He understood—and had long since come to terms with her desperate, crazy decision to have a child at any cost—but she wouldn't let him get a word in edgewise. Frustrated, he did the only thing he could to shut her up. He kissed her.

He tasted her surprise...and sudden, unexpected shyness. And just that easily, she melted his heart. "I thought I'd lost you, too," he murmured, kissing her softly, once, twice, then again. "When I saw Laureen with that knife, slashing at you, I felt as if she was ripping my heart out. All I could think was how much I loved you."

Stunned, she looked up at him with eyes that were suddenly swimming in tears. "You love me?"

"I've been fighting it ever since I met you," he admitted huskily. "I was just starting my practice. I'd already decided that I wouldn't get serious about anyone for at least a couple of years. Then there you were—this major distraction living right next door. I couldn't keep my eyes—or my hands—off you."

"I didn't think you were serious."

"I wouldn't even let myself consider the possibility that I was falling in love with you. I thought I had a handle on it. Then you didn't call, and everything changed."

Just thinking about how close he'd come to losing her still shook him to the core. With a murmur of need, he tightened his arms around her and pulled her close, kissing her with a tenderness that nearly destroyed both of them.

Tears pooled in her eyes and spilled over her lashes. "I love you, too," she said softly. "When I realized I was falling in love with you, I couldn't believe it. I didn't want to love you. I didn't want to love anyone."

"After what Jason did to you, sweetheart, I wouldn't blame you if you never trusted a man again in your life."

How could she have found a man who was so

understanding? Blinking back tears, she said, "I was just so afraid of getting hurt again."

"I know, sweetheart. But I can assure you I'm not going to hurt you. I'm not your ex."

"I know. But I want a baby," she said again. "And you're not ready to settle down. You said yourself the clinic takes a lot of your time. We're on two different paths, Turk. How—"

"Shhh." Not the least bit worried, he kissed her fiercely. "I'm not worried about the clinic, okay? We're doing great—everyone in town's welcomed us with open arms."

"But you said—"

"That I wasn't going to even think about getting married for a couple of years," he finished for her. "If I've learned anything today, sweetheart, it's that you can't plan life. I didn't plan Laureen. And I didn't plan falling in love with you any more than you planned falling in love with me, but it happened. Do you honestly think I'm going to walk away from that?"

A smile curled the corners of her mouth. "I was hoping you wouldn't."

"You're damn straight I'm not," he said with gratifying promptness. "When we met, all you wanted was a baby—or so you thought. I wanted more time—or so I thought. What we found instead was each other. How can that be wrong?"

With her heart pounding, he made her believe

that anything was possible. But there was still one thing they had left to discuss. "I still want a baby," she told him quietly. "I'm going to be thirty-six next month. If I wait two years to try to get pregnant, I'm afraid I never will."

"Okay."

"Okay? What does that mean? I need to know if you're ready to have a baby."

"Sweetheart, I love you. You're the one with the biological clock. This is your call. Whatever you decide is fine with me. But you have to decide now."

Surprised, she blinked. "Now? Why now?"

"Because I'm taking you to bed right now." And rising to his feet, he swept her up into his arms and started down the hall to her bedroom. Grinning when she looped her arms around his neck, he cocked a wicked brow at her. "Well? What's it going to be? You've got about twenty seconds to make up your mind."

"Twenty seconds, huh?" she chuckled.

"Eighteen," he retorted as he carried her into her bedroom. "Seventeen."

She'd have sworn she wanted a baby more than she wanted or needed her next breath, but in that instant, as he laid her on her bed and followed her down, she knew what was right for both of them. Without ever taking her eyes from him, she reached into the drawer of her nightstand and pulled out a condom. "I believe you're going to need this," she said huskily.

Surprised, he lifted a dark brow at her. "Are you sure?"

"I had a lot of time to think after we fought about my crazy plan to get pregnant," she admitted, "and I realized that it wasn't fair to me or a baby or my baby's father to rush into getting pregnant just because I'm afraid of running out of time. Three lives will be affected, and the timing has to be right for all of us. So I went out and bought a six-month supply of condoms."

"For me?"

"Of course for you! I love you! And I hoped…"

When she hesitated, he grinned at her sudden shyness and reached for the buttons of her blouse. "I hoped, too. So what happens at the end of six months?"

Her own fingers busy with his shirt, she smiled into his eyes. "I thought we could let nature take its course. Whatever happens…happens. If," she added with a flash of dimples, "that's okay with you."

"Hmm. I think I like the sound of that. Six months of condoms," he added with a grin. "Life doesn't get any better than that."

"Turk!"

Laughing, he kissed her fiercely. "Just kidding, sweetheart. Did I mention that I love you?"

"Yeah, right," she sniffed, fighting a grin. "You wouldn't know it by me. There's a whole box of condoms just sitting there, waiting to be used—"

"Really? Sounds like a throw down to me," he growled...and covered her mouth with his. Her laugh was swallowed by his kiss; there was no more time for talking.

Epilogue

Eight months later

Standing side by side at the kitchen sink, Rachel washed and rinsed the dinner dishes while Turk dried and put them away. He'd moved into her house the same day Laureen had tried to kill them both, but they no longer had to worry about her. She'd been convicted of stalking, assault and attempted murder. It would be years before she saw the light of day again without looking through bars.

Rachel seldom gave her a thought anymore. She and Turk had gone on with their lives, and she'd never been happier. Laureen was the past. They'd gotten married on Thanksgiving Day, and they couldn't have picked a more perfect day to begin their marriage. They had so much to be thankful for. Their love had only grown stronger over the past eight months, Turk's clinic was doing fantastic, and the bakery was open again and business was booming. Rachel couldn't remember ever being so happy.

"You're awfully quiet tonight," Turk said as he dried a plate and returned it to its place in the cabinet. "Something wrong?"

"Oh, no!" she said, flashing him a bright smile. "I was just thinking about our wedding and everything."

"Oh, yeah? Our wedding or our wedding night?"

"Both," she laughed, nudging him with her hip. "Have I told you today that I love you?"

"It seems to me you mentioned it this morning," he said with a grin. "But you can tell me again. I love you, too."

"I know." Her smile soft, she turned to give him a kiss. "So how was your day?"

"Busy. The flu's going around." Grimacing, he suddenly focused on her glowing face. "You must have had a good day. You went with Evelyn to the doctor, didn't you? How is she?"

"Fine," she assured him. "Her blood pressure and cholesterol are both down, and she's strong as a horse."

"Good. Anything else happen?"

"Not much," she said easily. Her eyes trained on

the skillet she was washing, she bit back a smile. "Oh, I forgot…there's a bun in the oven."

"No problem," he replied, and stepped over to the stove and pulled down the oven door. At the sight of the empty oven, he frowned. "No, there's not. You must have got it out already."

She giggled, only to quickly stifle the sound with her hand. "Sorry—I didn't. I couldn't."

"Why not? The oven's been off for an hour. It's not hot—"

Confused, he glanced up, right into her sparkling eyes. And just that quickly, understanding hit him right between the eyes. "You're pregnant."

Grinning, her eyes suddenly swimming in tears, she nodded. "I was afraid to hope. Turk! What are you doing?"

"Carrying you to bed," he growled as he swept her up into his arms. "Are you sure? Are you feeling all right? Have you been to the doctor?"

"I went to the doctor today, silly," she chuckled as he laid her on their bed and followed her down. "With Gran. I didn't want to tell you until I was sure. And I'm feeling wonderful! What about you? Are you okay with this?"

Okay? he wondered wildly. He'd just found out he was going to be a father. *Okay* didn't begin to describe the emotions churning inside him. Then his hand settled on her still flat stomach, his eyes met hers, and suddenly he couldn't stop smiling.

"Oh, yeah," he murmured, leaning down to give her a whisper-soft kiss that had the tears in her eyes spilling down her cheeks, "I'm more than okay, sweetheart. I'm going to be a father. Why didn't you tell me I'd feel this way? We could have done this eight months ago!"

Laughing, her eyes shining with love, she pulled him close for a fierce hug. "Then I guess we'll just have to do it again as soon as this little sweetheart is born. Did I tell you twins run in my family?"

Stunned, he gaped at her like a man who'd just been hit with a brick. "Oh, God!"

* * * * *

Turn the page for a sneak preview of
IF I'D NEVER KNOWN YOUR LOVE
by
Georgia Bockoven

From the brand-new series
Harlequin Everlasting Love
Every great love has a story to tell.™

One year, five months and four days missing

There's no way for you to know this, Evan, but I haven't written to you for a few months. Actually, it's been almost a year. I had a hard time picking up a pen once more after we paid the second ransom and then received a letter saying it wasn't enough. I was so sure you were coming home that I took the kids along to Bogotá so they could fly home with you and me, something I swore I'd never do. I've fallen in love with Colombia and the people who've opened their hearts to me. But fear is a constant companion when I'm there. I won't ever expose our children to that kind of danger again.

I'm at a loss over what to do anymore, Evan. I've begged and pleaded and thrown temper tantrums with every official I can corner both here and at home. They've been incredibly tolerant and understanding, but in the end as ineffectual as the rest of us.

I try to imagine what your life is like now, what you do every day, what you're wearing, what you eat. I want to believe that the people who have you are misguided yet kind, that they treat you well. It's how I survive day to day. To think of you being mistreated hurts too much. If I picture you locked away somewhere and suffering, a weight descends on me that makes it almost impossible to get out of bed in the morning.

Your captors surely know you by now. They have to recognize what a good man you are. I imagine you working with their children, telling them that you have children, too, showing them the pictures you carry in your wallet. Can't the men who have you understand how much your children miss you? How can it not matter to them?

How can they keep you away from us all this time? Over and over, we've done what they asked. Are they oblivious to the depth of their cruelty? What kind of people are they that they don't care?

I used to keep a calendar beside our bed next to the peach rose you picked for me before you left. Every night I marked another day, counting how many you'd been gone. I don't do that any longer. I don't want to be reminded of all the days we'll never get back.

When I can't sleep at night, I tell you about my day. I imagine you hearing me and smiling over the details that make up my life now. I never tell you how defeated I feel at moments or how hard I work to hide it from everyone for fear they will see it as a reason to stop believing you are coming home to us.

And I couldn't tell you about the lump I found in my breast and how difficult it was going through all the tests without you here to lean on. The lump was benign—the process reaching that diagnosis utterly terrifying. I couldn't stop thinking about what would happen to Shelly and Jason if something happened to me.

We need you to come home.

I'm worn down with missing you.

I'm going to read this tomorrow and will probably tear it up or burn it in the fireplace. I don't want you to get the idea I ever doubted what I was doing to free you or thought the work a burden. I would gladly spend the rest of my life at it, even if, in the end, we only had one day together.

You are my life, Evan.

I will love you forever.

* * * * *

Don't miss this deeply moving
Harlequin Everlasting Love story
about a woman's struggle to bring back
her kidnapped husband from Colombia and her
turmoil over whether to let go, finally,
and welcome another man into her life.
IF I'D NEVER KNOWN YOUR LOVE
by Georgia Bockoven
is available March 27, 2007.

And also look for
THE NIGHT WE MET
by Tara Taylor Quinn,
a story about finding love
when you least expect it.

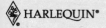

HARLEQUIN® *Romance*®

presents a brand-new trilogy by

PATRICIA THAYER

Rocky Mountain
BRIDES

Three sisters come home to wed.

In April don't miss

Raising the Rancher's Family,

followed by

The Sheriff's Pregnant Wife,

on sale May 2007,

and

A Mother for the Tycoon's Child,

on sale June 2007.

REQUEST YOUR FREE BOOKS!

2 FREE NOVELS PLUS 2 FREE GIFTS!

Silhouette® Romantic

SUSPENSE

Sparked by Danger, Fueled by Passion!

YES! Please send me 2 FREE Silhouette® Romantic Suspense novels and my 2 FREE gifts. After receiving them, if I don't wish to receive any more books, I can return the shipping statement marked "cancel." If I don't cancel, I will receive 4 brand-new novels every month and be billed just $4.24 per book in the U.S., or $4.99 per book in Canada, plus 25¢ shipping and handling per book plus applicable taxes, if any*. That's a savings of at least 15% off the cover price! I understand that accepting the 2 free books and gifts places me under no obligation to buy anything. I can always return a shipment and cancel at any time. Even if I never buy another book from Silhouette, the two free books and gifts are mine to keep forever.

240 SDN EEX6 340 SDN EEYJ

Name	(PLEASE PRINT)
Address	Apt. #
City	State/Prov.	Zip/Postal Code

Signature (if under 18, a parent or guardian must sign)

Mail to the Silhouette Reader Service™:
IN U.S.A.: P.O. Box 1867, Buffalo, NY 14240-1867
IN CANADA: P.O. Box 609, Fort Erie, Ontario L2A 5X3

Not valid to current Silhouette Intimate Moments subscribers.

Want to try two free books from another line?
Call 1-800-873-8635 or visit www.morefreebooks.com.

* Terms and prices subject to change without notice. NY residents add applicable sales tax. Canadian residents will be charged applicable provincial taxes and GST. This offer is limited to one order per household. All orders subject to approval. Credit or debit balances in a customer's account(s) may be offset by any other outstanding balance owed by or to the customer. Please allow 4 to 6 weeks for delivery.

Your Privacy: Silhouette is committed to protecting your privacy. Our Privacy Policy is available online at www.eHarlequin.com or upon request from the Reader Service. From time to time we make our lists of customers available to reputable firms who may have a product or service of interest to you. If you would prefer we not share your name and address, please check here. ☐

SRS07

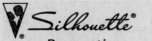

Romantic
SUSPENSE

COMING NEXT MONTH

#1459 DESI'S RESCUE—Ruth Wind
Sisters of the Mountain
Desi Rousseau was a suspect in her estranged husband's murder, and with the police willing to stop there, she resolved to get the answers herself. She wasn't prepared when hard as nails Tamati Neville offered to help clear her name, but she was desperate enough to take help wherever it was offered—and the fact that he was every woman's fantasy didn't hurt.

#1460 DIAGNOSIS: DANGER—Marie Ferrarella
The Doctors Pulaski
A pediatrician attracts the attention of an off-duty detective when she refuses to back down about her friend's death. Together they try to solve the mystery of his murder and discover that love can bloom in the strangest places.

#1461 THE PERFECT STRANGER—Jenna Mills
Detective John D'Ambrosia can't believe the woman he shared an incredible night with weeks ago is investigating the same case. Saura convinces him that he needs her to capture the villain, and against his better judgment he agrees. But can he survive his desire for his partner?

#1462 WARRIOR FOR ONE NIGHT—Nancy Gideon
When an undercover investigation leads Detective Xander Caufield to a charter security service, he isn't prepared for the onslaught of attraction for the woman assigned to "guard" him. Now he must battle his growing feelings for his protector…and potential suspect.

SRSCNM0307